BLOOD AND GUTS IN JAIL

ISAAC BJORN | a memoir

Blood And Guts In Jail by Isaac Bjorn

Made In Jail

Written by Mr. Isaac Bjorn. All Rights Reserved Copyright ©
ISAACBJORN & CO LIMITED

INTRODUCTION

Let me tell you how everything started. First of all I never seen myself a writer, it all started during the dead of December 2021. I was terribly bored in my own home. Only just finish producing my first ever personal piece of music, these days I also roll as PLANETBJORN, then I thought...well..what next? I then charged my iPad and wen't for a day out in the city centre of Glasgow. I end up in a cafe where I spent most of the day thinking what can I do to change circumstances in my life, but change them for the better. Well...there's nothing wrong with my life, everything is just fine, I'm healthy, fit, very much grateful i do what I do now and perhaps that's the most important...it's just I do want to push things further with my artist career for I feel too much time passed and not much happened. I just don't want to waste my amazing talent, my potential, by staying in the background for the rest of my life with such amazing skills I hold. There's quite a few good skills I hold...I can produce music, I can DJ, I can code, I can create NFT's...graphics, video... and that is a very good digital skill to hold these days. I can play quite a few instruments including reading and writing music. I speak three languages, English, Romanian and French. I'm quite good at solving problems...let's say on a consulting basis.....and apparently I can also write. However, here I am 30 years old in 2021 and absolutely nothing great happened in my life...still living in the background...alone, myself with myself. The light is very much dim in my life and I don't know why. Sometimes I think success it's never been meant to me. Here I was staying in the corner of that cafe and staring at an empty cup of tea, then, something happened, something came over me...and it was more like a state of mind, a mini depression, and I was very much aware of that. I then let that state of mind take full control of me. 100%. It was not pleasant at all. First time in my life I experienced depression. I can tell you now depression is a very ugly place to be. Have you ever watched Silent Hill? It's a movie (or a computer game). The character is trapped into a wasted city, lost,...but is also looking for a way out and all he can find around is just ashes, scary places, darkness all over the place, a lot of misery...truly a novel experience. That's how it is to live in depression. Very much a novel experience. There's also good novel experiences. This one wasn't. I'm mostly a happy person, I'm a people's person. I sometimes go live online and talk with my followers, stream my DJ sets over the internet, in between I talk about life, experiences, share what I know, help when I can, I'm quite happy who I am & what I am, but it was that moment in that cafe when that something came over me and I let it take full control of all my senses. When this state of mind took control of me I was fully aware everything was just an artefact of the mind, it was not real, it never existed but I just let it take full control of me. I then took my apple pencil and start putting down few ideas in my iPad and I done it in a way of how it will be like to imagine myself going thru the worst of things. A terminal illness perhaps? Not really. Too scary. I then looked into my life, especially my past...some events of my life if anything can relate to help me put down a story. Something to be guided from. There wasn't much events into my life to put down such a story and the only thing left was to just imagine one. I said to myself...well, I can sit down on the computer, open a music software and imagine...or think...look for an idea on how to write a song, anything really, and by the end of the day that idea took shape into something tangible (or intangible) but mainly I made it happen. Why not imagine a story and put it down on paper? I can do that. At that moment I really thought I can write a book. Perhaps a little one. Like one of those short novels...pocket books. And it clicked. Using this state of mind I charged myself 100% and give it a go to write something. I done it without even having the right experience. Mainly I learned the skill of storytelling in the process of doing it. I actually searched the internet what it takes to write a book and it says you need a special education, more like a degree in literature, even a PHD, MBA or something. I never heard of these things in my entire life. One man even told me that I need to be qualified to write a book. I then asked him...what kind of qualification I need...he said I need to finish a university. "You're out of your fuckin mind" I told him. My only qualification was this state of mind that took over me in a cafe just outside Glasgow's central station. It's not really a qualification... it's a tool that helped with putting down the topic of the book and the only way to make it happen was to imagine the worst of things happening in my life, then, a new beginning will start even if it was a total fiction. What I imagined you're about to see in a few pages from now if you dare to read further. Book idea put down at Glasgow's Bills cafe. Too bad they close it down. I really wanted to give them thanks for the free coffee. For now all I can tell you is that 'Blood And Gus In Jail' is an amazing story. It is a truly great memoir "wrote from absolutely knowing nothing about the story itself but just simply imagining the worst of things happening into my life." That's all. I believe I almost managed to do it even with almost no experience. It was a very difficult book to write. It took me exactly two months to write it plus an additional two to edit the whole manuscript. I'm now share it with you. It does contain some swearing...Sorry. Some dates are dated back to UK lockdown to merge with the characters and their story. Thank you for reading my book. If you find it interesting and you like it please tell me what you think on my tweeter feed. Author, Isaac Bjorn.

P.S: I did took a few hours of acting classes, learn the basics of script writing, learn how to create compelling plots, strong hooks, learn how to build an argument for the existence of fictional characters, and I even had to read books on Behavioural Psychology. I also had to learn about jail life in generally, and to do that I had to interview a few former prisoners. So I guess I'm quite qualified to write a book. What's next? A degree in literature to write the next? Tell me what you think.

My name is Saint Isaac, I am 30 years old and I'm currently living an unsuccessful life. I know, I know. I'm just a clown who's feeling down, except that I don't have clown shit to look like one

CONTENTS

Note

I really don't care what I will write. I'll just start with something and see how it goes and if indeed this story appears to be a total waste in the history of literature I still fulfilled the idea to create the moments I missed on the outside.

INTRODUCTION

You don't know about me and my heroine without you have read a book by the name of "Blood & Guts In Jail." I can assure you that my first book is indeed a good read. I talk about my life in jail and also about a disputed heroine that goes by the name of Julia, which neither cares nor exists, Julia just is. This book was wrote by Writer Isaac Bjorn. He did told the truth about me..."Saint Isaac" the one trapped between four imaginary walls...mainly. There is no evidence that I exist which makes perfectly sense that me & Julia are fictional characters. There were things the author stretched but he told the truth. I want to start with me first. As I previously said there is no evidence that I exist. I'm just a fictional character. Before I tell you about my troubles in jail I want to tell you what to expect in this book. It is important to read this book slow to enjoy a moment of laughter. That's all. This is one-of-a-kind story that has now become my own apocalypse of the past. If you haven't seen one yet, flip in and keep reading few more pages. You might like it. So, here's a story for you and it comes from the upper north of Scotland. Somewhere in the Shetland Islands. I believe is the perfect place to start a novel.

Done for drugs, both, distribution & consumption, I have received a mini-custodial-sentence for 100 days. Being first time in jail I have experienced an existential crisis with my life. Sometimes emotional and sometimes confusing. I describe it as fantastical descriptions and sometimes fanatical, encouraging a "drunk-and-drug-like-behaviour." A deadly effect that appeared to not be that deadly after all, instead, a crucial role in my writing. I will like to call it my historical account for writing behind bars. Unbelievable exciting stories, hundreds of them, relentlessly working my pen on paper, day and night keeping up with this flood of thoughts. In choosing to do so I have become a writer. On the outside I was absolutely nobody. I thought myself rather plain, the kind of person you might pass on the street or sit down next to on the bus without a second glance. Someone once told me that I am the kind of person you have to take a good look at to appreciate. And to tell you the truth I preferred fading in the background. Life is easier being unnoticed. Well, now I have this book...and there's also a second book coming which is the follow up from this one...so, I'll definitely be known for something. Apart from being a drug addict, I always been poor, homeless, on the road, moving places like a gypsy, going from job to job, addiction to addiction. I did tried to make a career in cooking. I wanted to become a chef. I failed badly. I also tried to become a musician, a record producer, a DJ. Unfortunately, in the end I failed at that too. Before i start writing this book my journey was totally different. For so long I was reduced to the extreme ashes of poverty, terrible mental health, and finally problem with the law which lead to where I am now...In jail. Hangout with the wrong people is just a plain answer. I can't do anything to solve this problem. I'm now in jail and that's it. Game over. Time on. A life of petty crimes that lead to a conviction. Prison took charge of my submissions. The not so lucky Saint Isaac, his life couldn't be much worse. In true context, during my time in jail, I have experienced extreme punishments, such as starving, extreme isolation and very bad mental health. Throughout this book you will get to discover some of that. There were also multiple mini suicide attempts and I don't know why all failed. Perhaps I'm blessed. The holly spirit looked after me. Somehow I managed to get out alive, travel the world and even write a second book. One more episode from my life utterly compelling. Fancy a quick look? Check out "Blood And Guts Before I Die," and see it for yourself. Theoretically, some of you will like it. Before I start telling my story I want to make one thing clear...I drive no particularly pleasure from operating with or against the crowd. I sometimes attack ideas not people. This book is a work of fiction and no event from it took place in real life. It did took place in an imaginary life. Written by Writer Isaac Bjorn. I think he done well.

PART I

Blood & Guts In Jail

2:19 a.m. I'm in my recording studio which is my living room and I so much love this room. It's the only place I feel the most complete. Synthesisers on my left side, drum machines on my right side, a pair of turntables in front of me. Hundreds of vinyl records all over the floor. I'm staring right now at all of them. It feels like an idealised utopian dream but complete. You might criticise it because it is unrealistic and shows a negative belief. I created my own fate. I stare at all this creative life found in my recording studio. I want to be part of it. The result of all this staring it can be hostile especially when I know I look at all my stuff for the very last time. For some reason I think I will go to jail in the next few hours. These coming days is going to be the worst of my days. I take a slow walk around my studio and gently touch my music instruments, my turntables, my speakers, my theory books and I flip thru them for the last time to remember those late nights when I was trying to learn my way thru them. It appears to be a total waste of time right now. I go in my book room to take a good look for the last time at my 997 book collection. My books were my mentors and guides. I shut down the light thinking how much I will miss them. I will miss my novella notes from the underground, self-help books, essays, and whatever is left behind...hundreds of books on specialised knowledge. Such a waste leaving all that behind. I go back in my recording studio and I go thru all my vinyl records. All of them. I count them all. But I do it in a rather disparate way to know they're all there. I guess it really doesn't matter anyway, everything it will be left behind in a few hours. I mean...my property it will stay here, but I will be going to jail for quite some time. I take a cloth and with a slow hand movement I clean the dust from a few of them. A side first, flip, B side after. My records are my beating heart. From a very young age I start collecting records. There were times in my youth when I was working a crap day job only for buying records. Can't believe I done that for more than a decade. Many didn't agreed with me. Many thought I'm insane...working only to save money to buy vinyl records. I thought is not true. I thought is my eulerian destiny, one day to become an artist, tour around the world and play all my records for people. Well, not really. Again, it appears to be a total waste of time. Counting done. 2991 vinyl records and it matches perfectly my numbers. My numbers are always right. Right? Right. God damn it...I'm such a pessimist. What's the worse than can happen to me...perhaps in prison for a few months, a few weeks, a few days? A community payback order. Anything is possible. My lawyer said If I'm found guilty I get the jail for sure and definitely two years. At least two years. Oh God...why all this happens to me! I can't resist two years in jail. Everything good I tried to create in my life...my creative life...everything that makes me happy it will be lost. When I get out of jail I'll be out and about on streets, homeless, dirty, begging and looking stupid...oh God, that's just not me. Reduced to the extreme ashes of poverty and from day one. Pretty much that's what jail will do to me. There must be another way to fix all this. Perhaps I could bargain with the judge. I could tell him that my fail as a citizen of this world can be fixed. I could change. I could become a better man. I could stop taking drugs. I could prove an exceptional character and try hold a good posture in the society. I simply failed for so long. I could try fix things. But the law doesn't offer excuses. The law is vulnerable yet self-assured and for some reason my gut tells me I get the jail. Damn it…I'm such a pessimist. Why I must always see the bad stuff. At least a bit of hope.

2:55 a.m. I'm at the kitchen table flipping randomly thru a book… "The Odyssey, by Homer." It appears to be the worst book to pick before going to jail. I don't know why I picked up this book. Perhaps is because I'm due for my annual leave…on a odyssey or something. It could be. I could also return home. It's possible. But just imagine tomorrow night at this exact time trapped between four dirty walls which will be my home for quite some time. A prison cell. Option A looks bad. I could also imagine tomorrow night at this exact time trapped between four beautiful walls surrounded by my vinyl records. My creative life. That will be so good. Option B looks good. Coming back home. It's just terrifying to think about option A: JAIL. Trapped between four ugly walls surrounded by…ugliness…I guess. My gut tells me is definitely going to be option B. Oh God…why on earth I'm such a pessimist. Why do I really have to trust my gut…I really want option B. Can you just make that happen? I'm trying to talk to God. The negative stuff always happens to me for some reason. Always does. I'm telling you…the bad stuff always happens to me. It just does and I really don't know why. I once read a book on behavioural psychology and it says that our thoughts becomes our words and our words becomes actions and actions becomes things that happens in real life. Imagine If you flip this simple equation on the positive stuff. Now we talking. Now we see the glass half full. Unfortunately not me. There's no room for the good stuff for a pessimist like me. Still, I don't think we are predetermined for the worst unless we chose to. Our actions are determined by our thoughts. I think we can chose to think more positive even in the most uncomfortable situations no matter how bad it can be. Yeah, right. I'm trying to stay positive before I go to jail. That's like trying to cheer-up things will get better before going to the guillotine. "Don't worry, everything is going to be fine, you'll just have your head cut off and that's all". Oh god... what on earth is with this distorted thinking. I'm literally a mess. God damn you Saint Isaac you're weak like a watermelon not anymore a special character. I feel like an expired pack of ham.

3:12 a.m. I open my laptop for the last time before I say good bye to it. I actually just recently bought it. My lately and newly macbook pro will definitely miss me. In the last few days I been working on a rather exciting project in a music software. Eventually I almost finished what I was trying...my very first piece of music. But I guess it really doesn't matter. It's all a waste of time. I close the project and click save. I don't know why I done that. Perhaps is because I will like to finish it when I'm out of jail. If I will ever be able to return home of course.

3:27 a.m. I'm back in my recording studio to play one more song before I drawn myself at sea with the mermaids. In this context...the mermaids being the prison guards. God I hate them. But I better be good with them otherwise they will badly fix my jail term. I can tell you more about that in a few pages from now. Finger crossed I go to jail so I can tell you more about my ugly experiences from jail. I'm only saying this in case you want to read my jail story. Are you with me? Good. And by the way...I'm just saying. But not because I want to go to jail but because I'm trying to write this book and apparently jail is the ultimate place to write a best seller. Yeah right...I could only wish. Personally, right now I prefer to be drawn at sea with my records but tightened around the edges of my neck. All of them. Wax is heavy I can tell you. I lit-up a cigarette and think. I stand up. I walk towards the shelfs and pick a record. I listen it very carefully, flipping between side A and side B but stoped anonymously on side B. It's Queen's Bohemian Rhapsody. It feels like life it just began to me. The record and my feelings clicked in me. Now I have to throw it all in. Open my secret drawer which is just under the floor, behind the cupboard more precisely. Over the past few months I managed to make a secret drawer in the floor is where I keep my drugs hidden from...anyone really. I take whatever is left and I do it...I will smoke my kif one last time. Going to jail anyway so it really doesn't mater. Pour out a glass of whiskey, lit-up my kif and I sprinkle on top of it some cocaine and a few drops of ketamine. I then burn a few pieces of hashish and sprinkle the bits on top of my kif. The result is...active ingredients that will make me forget I'm going to jail. I return to the turntable flip the record for side B and...another one bites the dust. Oh Freddie...I'm so ready for this. Warm-up a little with a few smokes then I trash myself on cocaine & alcohol. Gosh…is so good. I keep playing Freddie's record again & again. Side A. Side B. Keep switching sides. Ultimately I stop at…I want to break free. Oh my gosh…the cocaine and Freddie's voice smashed that LIKE button in my head. Fuck me. This is next level shit. This is cocaine speaking pouring freedom into me. I took my top off and start dancing around my studio. God knows how long this will last. Until my drugs will last. Oh I love my turntables. I love them so much. It's magic in the eyes to see the needle dancing on wax. Saint Isaac watch this carefully, it may be your last chance to trip on wax. You'll never know where you'll end up for the next few months. It's time to live the last dance.

3:59 a.m. I have exactly five hours until my time runs-out. At 9:00 a.m I have to attend court. So, assuming I'll be gone missing for a few months, responsibly I'll have a glass of whacky on thin ice. Cheers for that. For almost three hours I kept this cheerful attitude that everything is gonna be alright. I became very drunk, highly intoxicated on drugs and completely free from living in fear that I may be going to jail. I laugh at myself for almost three hours and the feeling was so good. It made my thinking that things could actually change for the better. Then the movie got broken. I stop the turntable, put back the record in the sleeve and back on the shelf where it belongs. I look at it for the last time. Gave a kiss on the sleeve, turn my back and said good bye. I start crying. It's okay to cry. I accept everything. This day has no accidents. I created my own fate. I'm crying…It's okay to cry.

8:16 a.m. I'm in my bedroom facing the cupboard. Highly intoxicated but still able to chose my best outfit. Unfortunately I only have two rounds of clothing. I wear the same thing every day. My white shirt, red bowtie and a gentlemen's suit that goes by the colour brown picked-up in a charity shop for £4.95. Apart from that I have one more pair of jeans, two t-shirts, two pairs of underwear, two pairs of socks, a jacket and a pair of boots. That's all my cupboard and I'm quite happy with this garderobe. I have made the conscious decision to wear my best suit. Wake up Saint Isaac you don't want to look stupid in the court room.

8:27 a.m. I'm out from my flat and it breaks my heart that It might be the last time I see it. I look one more time at my door, I enter the key in the locker, I lock the door and walk away. I felt so sad that I nearly threw the key away. Somehow I didn't. I kept my house key. Pocketed. On my way to the city and the sun is sunshine on me. Early November morning supposed to be grumpy. Not today. Outside still very cold. You'll never know how good that November sun was with me or was the drugs & alcohol dancing in me…Either way in an hour or so I'm fucked. I guess now I finally realised I might be going to jail.

8:47 a.m. Made it to Glasgow Sherif Court…It feels like I'm not in the right place. I hate this place. I hate it to death. I look in the reflection window from the main entrance to see my final mugshot. Looking like the perfect well dressed drug addict. I don't think I look like a criminal. I actually look very fashionable. I want to shout "I'm a celebrity get me out of here." Sorry, but I have a serious problem. The alcohol & drugs matured into me. Every minute I get more drunk and stoned in the same time. My vision is very unclear. I have a strange feeling that something rather weird I will do in the court room and that's not okay for my resume. I want to make it clear...I am very drunk and highly intoxicated at exactly 9:00 a.m. I'm doomed.

9:00 a.m. Right now I'm on a different vibe. Apart from being highly intoxicated I have become sick...possibly in a sensation of vomit. I feel like this will go as the most unpleasant experience in the history of literature...more like a bad trip. I'm losing the ability to know the difference between what is real and what is not. Quickly went to the bathroom and took whatever was left on me... 5000 micrograms of LSD. I make my way into the court room at exact 9:11 a.m awaiting for my crash date. As the acid took over I went full potatoes.

9:11 a.m. Jesus Christ...this court room is in chaos style. What is going one here? I feel alienated by my companions...a couple of onions drags me into the court room. The floor was melting and churning and my jury looks like a comic book filled with animated characters. The judge is painted on a field and it looks more like a Van Gogh painting. Everything in my field of vision it looks slabbed, more like one of his paintings. For some reasons the judge's behaviour felt out of control. He doesn't move. Is stoned in the painting. Flat. Completely muted, although he looks briefly sobered in a indecent exposure with his toe. I feel like everything is breathing and coming at me or is just my drop of acid taking life slowly inside me. It could be. I want to go home please. I want to have a walk in the park. Enjoy a theatre with theme music and make beautiful gestures at pigeons. I want to stop at my local record shop, pick up some records, have a haircut and enjoy an espresso at my favourite restaurant. I also want to have a croissant on my way out. I want to end up my day celebrating the end of my song. I want to climb the ladder of success in the escalator style. And I want to do it on Spotify. I want a big question only for me: Am I going to be missing for the next few months? Live incredible adventures on the road and use my own personality to write a book that will eventually win peoples hearts? I'm over the moon if that's true. The story is just about to begin.

9:23 a.m. It's been more or less ten minutes and the characters from the court room start moving. Oh wait a second…the judge just moved. I thought is stoned. Is just fixing his toe. I'm placed in the dock facing his toe. Still highly intoxicated. I walked on top of a chair and with my head held high I shouted loud…"I have a hangover." I then vomited and fell on the floor. I'm pretty sure I hit my head very badly. Heck…I'm not even mad…that's amazing. "Not a good start but keep going." — The judge said. "Damn it. You pooped out from the painting? How'd you do that?" I asked the judge. "You're so wise. You're like a miniature Buddha, covered with hair. I freakin' love you judge!" "I'm sorry champ"— The judge said. "I think I'm sending you to jail but not for too long but for one crazy adventure... what do you think?" The judge said. "Tell me more about this jail, judge, by the way...you look classy...Hey judge?This is one crazy party. Will you join me?... and just for the record I have a hungover. Can you forgive me? I'm also very important. I have many leather-bound books in my book library. And my apartment smells of waxed records." "Tell me about it"— The judge said. "What do you say if we get you in your jail pyjamas and hit the cell for a few days? Bedtime? You look tired young man!" "Okay, let's do it." I said "You mean you wanna go to jail for a few days?" — The judge said. "I'm sorry judge...I think I don't like the jail. I changed my mind." "Oh... I'm sorry champ. I think I have the perfect place for you"— The judge said. "Really? Where? "Well let's keep it a surprise for now. You'll love it there!" "Awesome..." I said. "I'm going on an adventure" "Oh yes you will young man. You definitely going to be on the adventure of your life time. But you need to map out the stories you're going to write, perhaps enlist a few adventure buddies to accompany you on the journey. I hope this adventure will encourage you to get going with your book. You did said you gonna write a book did you?" "I did Judge. I did." My book is gonna be a best seller. "Good stuff young man. Here, let me sort out the numbers for you. I'm giving you no more than 100 days in jail and this shod encourage you to write your book. Sending you to Shetland's finest jail." "Are you serious man? You send me to jail? I'm only tripping a little." The drugs & alcohol melted so badly in me. I felt like I could become absolutely anyone. I had one of those faces — the ready smile that suggested I was an open book, someone who had no secrets to keep and if I did I wouldn't be able to keep them anyway. My real problem now is that I'm going to jail for the next 100 days. Am I tripping or is only real?...And what on earth is this place... Shetland....Never heard of it. God help me what's going to happen to me next. This is getting real. I'm out of the courtroom heading to jail.

8. 11. 2019: It was sunny when I left the flat. It is cloudy when I left the court. It will be dark when I will be arriving in jail. Last night I was in for a treat. Today I'm all in for the hell of my life. Been told by the court officer that jail food is served once a day and is barely sufficient in nutrients and is engineered to be that way so it can put me in shock. Am I right? I don't know. Soon I find out. Stay tune for stories that will get you shocked. Oh god...the shit I got my self into... and for what? For flipping cocaine on street corners for minimum wage...unbelievably embarrassing. This will go terribly bad on me. At least if I was doing more than £50 a week. Sorry, those were better days. Usually a tena now and then...those were my days. How embarrassing. I admit. I was poor. I was in a terrible need to have money for food. And there were also the bills...electricity, gas and all that. Mostly I flipped drugs on street corners only when I had to pay the bills. That's the truth. Now in jail. That's also true. Amongst all these inconveniences and annoyances I couldn't help wonder how my cell will look like. I know jail cells look like shit. Four walls and a bed. A toilet to shit in and a sink to drink...jail water. Yuck. It sucks. I'm thinking how to make my life easier in jail. I know. I'll just write a letter to the governor and I'll ask him for a favour. I

once heard on the internet that first time offenders receive first time favours. If this is true then I will like please to sign-up in advance for high speed internet. And I want the full fibre, the one that says on TV. I also want to receive books...stuff like Nabokov, Dickens, Kathy Acker, Highsmith, Marcel Proust, and I want them all brand new. And I also want a daily newsletter from my favourite DJ Magazine to keep up with the latest from the music scene. If possible I also want a stereo player with unlimited CD's, bags of peanuts, a pot of Creme De La Mer to keep my skin nourished, eye cream from La Prairie with three complimentary samples of skin caviar and I also want Sisley's latest Black Rose Mask to keep my skin glowing for the rest of my jail term, some comic books, tattle and soul. Having all this stuff within a few hours I'm all set with the jail system and will also produce a substantial amount of work for my book. So, I now have a plan put in place. The temperature had dropped nearly to zero and I can tell by looking out the window. I see some rather small particles of frost glued on the window. By evening I landed in Scalloway. It appears to be a small town on Shetland's mainland. They brought me in a tiny aeroplane. Glasgow it appears to be quite far. I don't even know where I am. In hell probably. "You have to understand what Shetland is like," says Fraser, my prison guard. "We're pretty isolated, surrounded by sea. I'm sure you have nowhere to go if you manage to run away." Motherfucker...he read my thoughts. Who's this fool, a psychic or something? "I think you'll enjoy your time in Shetland" — the officer said. "Welcome to Shetland's Drug Rehab Hospital. Also jail for the ones who flew over the cuckoo's nest. "I thought I'm going to jail...what on earth is this place? I didn't sign up for staying with crazy people. "Don't worry"

— the officer said. "It's pretty much the same like any other jail. You'll get your cell, your meal and most important you'll get your meds. Happy life." Yeah, fuck off, I said in my head. Not really. It makes it very scary. However, in the same time I never been so excited to see what's inside this place and how it will look like. I believe this is one of the contributing factors to my anxiety that eventually help me write my book. If it looks bad I just want to be under the blanket, covering my ears and humming the tune to Bruce Springsteen's "Pink Cadillac." From the outside the building looked just like any other hospital, but there was one thing that I thought is strange… all windows have metal bars, pretty much like in jail. I enter the jail reception and seen these complete white corridors which I thought was quite strange. Absolutely everything was white. For a moment it affected my eyes. The neon light and the corridors felt like a burn in my eyes. Made me terribly distressed. Clinical white walls and very ugly smell all over the place. I think is the smell of death if that's something that exists in the Oxford dictionary. If not then I believe I score it first. I had a long walk with the guard until I arrived at assessment office. The door says "risk assessment." I enter inside. A rather cosy room. After ten minutes of all sort of distressing questions and a whole row of unlimited paperwork done on me, the doctors' conclusion was that I suffer from sour grapes syndrome and for the next 100 days I need to take a treatment. He stamps the paper marked "sour-grape effect." I don't even know what that means. These motherfuckers are going to do experiments on me. It also says at the bottom of the paper I was a suicide risk and needed to be admitted to 24 hours-a-day care to feel extremely good. This is bullshit. I'm not feeling at all suicidal. I just done cocaine.

At short notice I was escorted to another wing of the building where a door slammed shut and locked behind me. That's where everything kicked in. I encountered the real jail effect on me. This is the real deal where crazy people live. I'm now part of them. For the night I was confined inside a white room with high walls and absolutely no window. It felt weird. I could not believe I'm in such a place. Few minutes later a lady opens the door saying is time for my meds. I follow her. The air on the corridor was stiflingly weird and smelled of unwashed bodies and cooking. Men and women roamed the halls aimlessly, some screamed and some shouted after something I couldn't understand while others stared into the distance with an alarming lack of awareness. What a fuck is going on here...I keep ask myself. What am I doing here. Passing by another corridor and seen some other patients...or prisoners that looked like the normal well-dressed types you'd see on any high street — but others wore filthy clothes and were extremely dishevelled. By the way, some patients behaved. It became apparent that some were suffering with far more than just depression. I was surprised that people with different mental illnesses were grouped together. I supposed to be safe here, yet I had everything I needed to inflict serious personal damage. In all honesty I was frightened beyond belief. I felt a need to calm my nerves so I asked if I could go outside for a cigarette. A casually-dressed nurse pointed to a door which led to a small cramped outdoor cage. Chain link prison fence all over the place that includes above my head. For fucks sake...this place is weird. The moment I entered the smoking area two female patients, both appeared to not be that old, perhaps in their thirties or forties, they both followed me. I was shocked by their stained clothes, unwashed hair and filthy hands. They began to paw at me…one strike me on the back of my head with her shoe. I asked them to stop. They didn't. They forced me into a cramped corner blocking my escape. Both demanded my cigarettes. I told them to fuck-off and to leave me alone. But they didn't listen and become aggressive. One of them spat me straight in my eyes. The other spat me contemptuously right in the face. Here I am cornered and spat at all over by crazy people. "You tried to take my cigarettes" — one of them shouted. She sounded foreign. Eastern European or something. I then start shouting too. "Fuck off bitch, they are mine, not yours. Get the fuck off from me. Leave me alone" — I shouted back. I pushed the door behind and showed them the middle finger with both of my hands. And in the same time I also shouted…"you fuckin ugly bitches…a big fuck you." I believe in doing this myself I become part of the cuckoos tribe. Checking the smoking area I see no sign of them. They left. Finally had my cigarette and tried to forget about the concerns. I was concerned what I will face for the next 100 days. Probably all kind of strange stuff. Strange stuff will also end up in my book then. So be it. But this is definitely not the place I shod be. "Your room is ready now" — a doctor said, and he pointed me in my room. I mean in my cell. At least it was clean. It contains a single bed, wardrobe, sink, toilet…and by the way I think is disgusting sleeping with a toilet in your room…actually this is a cell so I better get used to it. There's also a desk and a chair. No TV. No internet. No cd's, no books, definitely no potions and lotions. And no mirror. Weird. I tried to complain but no hope. "Everyday I'll need to look through your things and take anything that might be dangerous so you not gonna hurt yourself"— the doctor said. Within seconds of being locked in my cell, male & female patients swamped the glass window to stare at me. The two ugly bitches came back and start making strange gestures at me. They all looked like some kind of alien creatures from another planet. I was too afraid to sleep from too much shouting, patients from another cells start scramming. All kind of strange noises. I lay down and pulled the blanket over my head. Moments later my door was kicked by something hard. I think it was a chair or something. It was a woman with a very ugly face. She screamed…glaring at me…"This is my room" —she said. "Fuck-off," I said to her. I didn't bother to explain. Explain what? To crazy people…no thanks. It didn't took too long and a nurse wearing all white clothing came to tell me it was dinner time. Great. And in the same time it will be interesting to see what these weirdos eat. By now I was constantly shaking with nerves. She told me eating would make me feel better. Yeah right. That's a big bullshit. In the canteen now and I see plenty of patients queuing for food. Patients and prisoners combined. The whole gamut of insanity was here and I was with them too. Can't believe this is actually happening. Listening to their chatter I was shocked to discover that some had been living in these premises for more than two decades. Jesus Christ. I think they just kept them here for as long as doctors want to. Looking at these characters even after two decades had no real success in getting better. All of them looked brain burned. Seems to me like they enjoy here because some make jokes and laugh very hard. At the kitchen window now and I received a huge mound of potatoes covered with a red sauce and bake beans on top. A bowl of soup too, and with a green like texture. Looking inside the bowl it looked perfectly like a fluid liquid of alien blood. Oh lord help me. It was difficult for me to eat that crap. I tried to look at others to believe is eatable and follow spoon in, spoon out. It's hard to see how anyone could start to feel better on this diet. No wonder everyone here is fat and ugly. The woman who claimed I had stolen her room glared at me with ferocious intensity. She and several others noisily making fun of me. One of them pointed her ass towards me and farted in my face. I can't believe this shit actually happened to me. But when she pointed her ass towards me it happen to see her underwear and I'm not saying this because I intentionally wanted to see them but because she pulled down her pyjamas and I swear I seen a brown stain on her underwear. Probably the last time she wiped her ass was quite some time ago. How on earth these characters can function in a civilised society. I may be a little unwell, but I will never ever behave in such a way in a civilised world. Took my plate and went in the back. Chosen the most far away table and had my food there. Spoon in, spoon out and in between I start crying. Just couldn't understand what am I doing here. Not the place I shod be. Seems to me I will have a hard time here for the next 100 days. "Everyone in their rooms" — the nurse shouted. Good, I said. It will be a nightmare to be here longer than five minutes. Shaking and tearful I went back to my cell. On the way back to my cell the doctor explained me that the wing I am right now is perfectly fine for my staying and I shod not be that worry. "Fuck-off"— I told him. "I ain't sick at all. Look at these characters. They are the ones who are sick and needs help not me. I'm perfectly okay." I asked to leave me alone and to have my door locked so I can be safe during the night. I even thought to sleep with something under my pillow, a hammer or something just in case I'll be attacked by one of these weirdos. There wasn't anything available to grab. 99 days left. Looking forward to get out this fuckin place.

9. 11. 2019: Woke up and feel like shit. Some strange pain all over my body. My vision is blurred. Must be the meeds they gave me. I'll probably become one with the whole gamut of weirdos found in this place. I was gobsmacked to see a very ugly woman licking the window of my cell. Seeing that shit just made all the drugs kicking out from me. She is shouting at me thru the window saying I am the kind of person she is attractive and she wants to fuck me. I shouted back…"You are fucking ugly…fuck off from my window." She didn't left. She start shouting even louder saying I am young, attractive and looking professional and I generate curiosity to her cunt. I stand up, took a chair and hit the window so badly that I thought I crashed it all over the place. It didn't. It was one of those secure windows that can't crash, but the bitch run away. That did explained why I was punished for the day by the governor. I now have a report on my file. I did tried to explain what made me to smash that chair in the window, however, I was in a crazy peoples place and accordingly treated pretty much the same. Crazy. Just had a new drug prescribed. Its called Lorazepam — a drug used to treat anxiety. I swallowed a couple of pills at once. I settled back into my room trying to do some writing but no joy. The drugs kicked in me and I feel rather sleepy for the rest of the day. How utterly terrifying is this place. God help me get out alive from this hell. Every drop of thought where I am right now is rubbing thru my head thinking what on earth I will write in my book. I suppose to go to jail not in hell. What will my

readers think. Fuck it. I'll just go with whatever happen next, write about the stuff that happens to me. And I'll do it with precision so everyone will get to know what I'm going thru. Somehow a story will follow next. So what's next? The substance of hell. By the way, one day I could become famous for my writing. Why? Look where I am. Oh hey…wait to see where I go next. Keep reading.

10. 11. 2019: It's Sunday. Over the next several hours I'm due for a series of medical challenges. I been told I'll be put on the doctor's drug of choice… benzodiazepines. This drug is bad news for my creative mind. It will act as a sedative for the rational thought, slowing down thinking functions. It reduces dramatically the brain activity in the areas of the brain responsible for rational thought. Can you believe this shit? I'm going to be brain washed. Rational thinking is crucial for writing my book. I must have the ability to consider the relevant variables of a narrative, access, organise, and analyse information for my book such as facts, opinions, judgments, and data and to arrive at a sound conclusion in line with my writing. I need to be healthy. I don't want to become like one of these weirdos, all day walking dead on the corridors. Like a zombie or something. Brainwashed from a cocktail of drugs. I think it would be accurate to say to myself I will become too…a walking dead writer? Becoming addicted to the process of melting away into nothingness. Eat. Sleep. Repeat. Taking meds. Eat. Sleep. Repeat. Taking meds. This is also bad news for my book. Perhaps I shod name my book "Eat. Sleep. Repeat. Taking. Meds. Getting in the jail routine." I expect to be

active with the desire to be present in my writing. For Saint Isaac everything is possible.

11. 11. 2019: Last night I had a ton of issues piled on top of me. Most of the night I had problems with sleep, emotional regulation, imaginary conversations and other things popped up, however, suddenly I thought about my girl…Julia. The love of my life. Yes, I do have a girlfriend. She's more better than me in any circumstances. She ticks all the boxes of a successful life. Sometimes I don't know why she hangs out with a loser like me. I will never forget when she told me why…"because I believe in you my love, you will become someone one day…you're truly special and because of that I love you." Now those are nice words you don't get to hear that often from a partner. But is me who's always a dick head with her. Why?" Because I don't believe in me. Because I believe I am destined for failure. Always. Here I am in jail…It's more than a simple proof. Last night in my dream she provided me with new coping tools to use to help me stay grounded, sane, and on fire for 100 days in jail. By early morning I felt a bit more comfortable in my own skin. With her help I'm hoping every day to grow a little stronger. Actually, I feel a bit more better right now despite the stingy drug I took earlier…it kinda slows down my brain activity. I think I can keep going. Going for a ciggy and later on will write down a few thoughts about how I feel. I'm just outside in the exercise yard and I'm immediately met with a blast of Shetland wind. Cold as fuck and is rather an-artic-like-wind. I wrap my neck with a blanket from my room… oh god it smells so bad. It remembers me of that ugly woman who happens to

fart in my face. What a fuckin woman. Finished my ciggy and came back in. I passed the TV room and on my way to my cell I see a woman masturbating. She's doing it on the corridor. What a location to fuck yourself. Oh dear. She placed a spoon in her cunt...spoon in, spoon out and from time to time she is licking the spoon in her mouth then she is inserting the spoon back in her cunt. Quite rapidly like there's a specific interest in the taste. Now that is a totally fucked-up thing to do. And she's also staring at while she's sucking her cunt with a spoon. Doing that shit on the corridor is just sick. She's following me in the smoking area. Can't believe how ugly she is. She smells like death. More like a cadaver left for a week under a blasting sun. I better keep the distance. Pretended I go back in then went straight out in the smoking area to get rid of her. Light up another ciggy to try fade away some of my anxiety. I feel shit really. Finished my smoke and went back in. Been told it's time to take my meeds. If I don't take them I get punished. What can I do...comply with the rules. Try survive this hell and eventually...hopefully one day get out and try live life. I'll probably go straight for bed after my meds. They will make me sleepy anyway. Hopefully I'll still be alive next day.

12. 11. 2019: Why does anyone write their own stories? Anyone can write but not everyone will write a story that everyone wants to read. It is a question I keep ask myself several times a day while working on mine. The last 24 hours were pretty much just as insane as the night before last nigh. I'm trying to get along with the jail days. I have found them to be quite hard. I once read somewhere in a magazine that jail could be the perfect place to write some

interesting stuff. You have material to write about. To be honest some of the best books in history has been wrote in jail. Fyodor Dostoevsky is the perfect example. And jail in 1800's Russia looked really bad. Nurse came in and being told to go for my meds. It's now been twice and is only mid day. The nurse is looking at me to make sure I swallow them. Then I'm being asked to open my mouth and she's taking a good look to make sure I don't hide them or something. Went back to my cell, pulled of some paper and wrote a letter to my girl.

Dear Julia,

...damn it. I only managed to write the title of the letter then the pencil got broken and I have nothing else to write. Maybe another time. God damn it...I need to write her. I need her in my life. She is strong and severe and everything I am not. Fuck sake...I just dropped my toothbrush in the toilet. It's okay. I'm in jail. Anything is possible. In jail there are bad days and there are legendary bad days. This day is in between the two. I found this explanation to be considered as the only one. Earlier today while I was staying in bed I confess I have heard a bunch of sounds that were high-pitched similar to crickets but everything was rather strange because there aren't any crickets in the winter time, however, it could be the meeds creating deadly moments of despair and my mind what else can do but just wander in the search for them. Today I overlooked the sea and the wind carried the smell of my beautiful girl into my two meter cubicle home. It appears to be a rare form of inspiration for my writing. Hopefully I'll write something better in the coming days if I'm still sane and in the right mind.

13. 11. 2019: This fuckin place is dull. Very grim. They moved me in a separate wing of the building. Two prison officers came very early in the morning. Told me I have five minutes to pack my stuff and escorted me out of the building. Apparently is because I'm being considered vulnerable to the rest of the weirdos and is for my own safety to leave that wing. Very quiet here where I am now, no sounds, just the birds. Birds are sometimes coming by my window. I think I'm alone in this part of the building. Suddenly is nigh. I nearly lost the count of time. Cell door gets closed behind and what else can I do but just to lay in bed half dead. Physically and morally I'm not well. I feel very sad. The moon is glamorous tonight. From inside the cell in pitch black I look at it. It is more like a lamp. How astonishing is this night. You see…if I wasn't in jail I would never see this moon light. Such a point. Don't you think? Not much to see outside but just the usual country side landscape and the harbour facing the north sea. Looking at the moon and its position in the sky I assume is no later than midnight. I mark this entrance in my diary. It is important for me to keep an account about time. These motherfuckers even took my TV. I only have a bed, a chair, a desk, and my diary and a bunch of pencils. For some reason they intentionally gave me a bunch of pencils. I think by now they know I am a writer. Oh god…I forgot to mention the toilet. A hole in the floor going fuck knows somewhere. And of course the jail clothes…the stuff I wear now which is disgusting. My jail clothing smells bad. They are heavy and causes a rash all over my body. Motherfuckers are punishing me. I look at the moon again and its position in the sky

moved slightly to the right. It is now 1:00 a.m I think. It is important
for me to keep track of time until I find out a way out from this hell.
Soon to be the modern life of Saint Isaac in jail. Keep reading for I
keep writing. I mark again this entrance in my diary. It is important
for me to keep a record of Saint Isaac's diary. Looking at what I
wear it's a fuckin joke. Orange jail clothing. Fuckin disgusting.
There's just too many questions to be asked about this ugly clothing
and why the hell I am wearing them, because on the other side of the
building I was wearing my own clothing until they moved me. This cell
is even smaller. Two meters square cubicle I think. I mark again this
entrance in my diary. It is important for me to keep a record of
what's happening in my cell. The cell itself is filthy and smells very
bad. Oh god it smells so bad. The smell is very specific to prison,
more like a combination of chlorine and urine, some ammonia in
between and dirt notes on top. If you never smelled this weird
combination then don't. Very bitter smell. It does leave a
psychological mark on you. Sorry, I mean on me. Not you. Just
clarifying. Looking back on these notes or odour or whatever the hell
is, I'm thinking to propose a deal for a new perfume and I'll do it
when I get out of jail. I actually know a French house that does
perfumes, it's down town Paris. If they ask me for a sample I'll just
use my jail clothing to justify the scent. It will do. I actually thought
about the name for my new perfume. "Saint Isaac — No5." I mark
again this entrance in my diary. It is important for me to keep a
record of how to quickly start a legit business when I get out. This is
no locker-room-talking. This is my meds talking. I told you it only
takes me a week or less to get in line with the weirdos. Oh god…this
smell. It is printed all over the place. In the walls. In the floor. In the

toilet. Even in my clothing. That's very unhealthy and annoying in the same time. A very tiny window the size of a football is located on the upper wall facing north and is all the air and view I have. There's a sink with tap water and that's good. I'll need to drink water. The sink is looking dirty. The toilet doesn't have a lid. Some water is dripping at all time from a pipe located under the sink and all this it makes my staying in jail very uncomfortable. The bed is a full metal frame with a mattress on top and some blanket that smells so bad. It smells just like the toilet, that bad is the smell. The blanket is very dull, heavy and uncomfortable. I fear of bed bugs and more rashes on my skin. A very bright light at all time which is typical for the jail cell is missing. I do enjoy staying in the dark and the moon light it feels good so far. It makes my night alright. One good thing so far. I mark again this entrance in my diary. It is important for me to keep a record of what's happening around my cell that includes every moving organisms such as bugs, rats, mosquitos and other creatures, myself included. I'm becoming very emotional almost to achieve a state of panic attack that's because I feel so lonely. Some steps on the corridor and is approaching my door. It was a prison officer. He pinched his eyes in to see what I am doing then he left. I wanted to ask him for a ciggy but left very quickly. I'm having a hard time to understand what's happening. Perhaps everything is happening now is only a nightmare, a very ugly dream and when I wake up everything will be back to normal. Yes, perhaps I'm dreaming. I'm now home in my bed sleeping very deep from a dose of heroine and god decided to show me the consequences if I keep taking drugs. I slap my face once. Twice. It appears I am very much awake and in jail. Very much awake and conscious of all my shit. My nightmare is only real. I mark again this entrance in my diary. It is important for me to keep a record of how I feel. But there's also version two of this ugly dream. Perhaps I am indeed insane and someone locked me here in this ugly place and all this actually happens for real. But that can't be true. At home I live a highly creative life. I make music. I DJ. I go to cinema. I go hiking. I have a girlfriend too. I live a normal life…I am a good person and don't deserve this. I'm not a criminal. "Hello? Anyone? Someone? Is there anyone here? Please let me out. I want to go home." No one around. Not even a step on the corridor. Not even a simple… "Are you okay young man? Do you need anything? A glass of water?" Perhaps a cigarette? You know…the simple stuff. Advice? Never come to jail. You heard me? Don't get the jail. You will suffer. Yes you will. I mark again this entrance in my diary. It is important for me to keep a record of how I feel. There's a tiny space under the door and I tried to take a look if anyone might be around. The corridor it seems to be completely empty also pitch black, absolutely no one around, no lights, no sign of humans. No sounds. Quiet. I now actually prefer a little noise. I was better with the whole gamut of insanity on the other side of the building. At least there I could see people around. There was a TV room. An exercise yard. Smoking area. I was free to go out from my cell during the day. I guess it was alright. Definitely better than where I am now. Here is disgusting. I'm telling you. I'm being punished. This is a test to see how I deal under pressure. I take the chair and hit the door very hard in the hope to attract someones attention but nothing happened. I hit the door again and this time with the hope to smash it. Solid jail door made from metal. No hope. No sound of footsteps on the corridor. I'm hungry, thirsty and very anxious and I look for answers to understand what the hell is going on here. I look again at the moon and somehow I calm down. I felt an escape into its kindness just by looking at the moon. It's like she whispers me to lay down in bed with incredible thoughts. Ambitiously and positively I did just that. Like a snake I immediately snook myself in that uncomfortable bed but somehow I managed to imagine it cosy and waiting for daylight. Without a clue I'm now on a bipolar expedition waiting for daylight. Before I fell asleep I imagined my books and my vinyl records...they were my sole companions to live a better life. My creative life.

14. 11. 2019: Woke up terribly sick and very depressed. The worst day of my life...I just can't imagine something more worse than waking up in jail and facing an ugly wall, horrible smell and the only place to go is back to bed. That is a horrible way to live life. If I ask myself ..."not sure what's wrong with me"...then this is what's wrong with me....the fuckin jail effect on me. But there are more bad news... About mid-day a prison guard found me almost unconscious on the floor. I hit my head against the wall until I start bleeding. I was taken in a rush to see a doctor at the jail hospital. Apparently they have an emergency unit available locally. The doctor said I am sick and I need immediate mental health treatment. He told the guard to let me stay for a day or two in the hospital to get better. I been diagnosed with Autism which is something that I lived with all my life but the jail made it even worse for me. After one hour I been incarcerated and sent back to my cell. The officers simply refused to let me stay in the hospital for a night. It was for my own good to simply just get better.

Before I left the hospital the doctor gave me a small packet which I hid under my jumper. When I arrived back to my cell I was so excited to see what's inside... I quickly open it. Found half a bread, some cheese, a small jar of marmalade and best of all a bar of chocolate. There was also a soap too. You not gonna believe how happy I was. Happiness in a packet.

On the outside stuff like that I always took it for granted. Now in jail I'm incredible grateful for these little things. The little things that matter. I eat the bread and the cheese and flip the whole jar of marmalade in between and in ten seconds everything disappeared down the throat. Life just got better for the time being. Kept the chocolate for latter. At first I was very ill, now, suddenly just got better. My strengths returned to me. About the evening time I received my first ever jail food and it's disgusting. I learned that jail food is different in this wing than the other wing. I really don't know why. Maybe is because I'm being terribly punished. Today's jail food is a plate of thin porridge made with cold water and one piece of black bread. Found all this stuff on the floor. Horrible. Came back in bed and had the bar of chocolate received from the doctor. Thrilled to find it contains some biscuits. Bright-white chocolate sauce and the biscuit under. I eat it in five seconds and my faith in God restored instantly. It gave me comfort and strength. Also wonderful news for my writing. I'm about to write a letter to my girl. This time I want her to know something she might have missed from my previous letter. The previous letter end up in the bin. Well…the pencil got broken. Such an excuse. It turns out she hated me in the past. Better write her and try correct things.

Dear Julia,

I must write you again to correct things between me and you because I think the last letter went out quite wrong. Actually let me correct that. The previous letter end up in bin. Thank god my pencil broke otherwise I'll post something to you that will make you hate me. Today I've come to my senses and this is accidental. Earlier I wanted to end my life. I wanted to sweep myself off the earth like a vile insect then I realise I will lose my beautiful mind. What's the point one to take his own life when has so much to offer for the world? I believe I have a beautiful mind and I want to share it thru all my work when I'm out of jail. And you know what? I might need a place to stay in 100 days or less for I truly think I'm homeless due to not paying my rent. Since in jail I have been spending my time with writing letters. I believe is a great practice before start writing a book. Most letters were for you...I mostly imagine losing you...then wanting you back...then loosing you again and so on. You know why? Because you're the most beautiful girl I have ever seen since you saved me from the streets. I say this emphatically because I love you. Cable me softly girl and tell me how much you love me. Yours, Saint Isaac

15. 11. 2019: I've been reading and re-reading all day an old Gideon Bible especially the James's section and some parables from Jesus. What else would you like me to do in this ugly cell...other activities? Yes...I know one. Staring at a blank wall. At leats it will make sense since I am in a weirdos place. Yes...about the Bible. Parables and my thoughts on God. It has come to my senses that the life and suffering of Jesus became more real to me than ever before. I even began to see that all my suffering might have a purpose. The death of Jesus had brought forgiveness to mankind. In the same way I feel God can bring something good out of troubles. This thought gave me fresh courage and strength. I mark this entrance in my diary. It is important for me to keep a record of my thoughts. Gosh...there's so much jail time to go. I can't wait for that day when I pack my

belongings and march the gates of hell. Actually I have not much but just what's on me...the jail clothes. The few bits I came with are kept at the reception jail. Other activities for today? Apparently I keep dream about wonderful news from my girl. Hoping to receive a cable from her. I'm feeling very lonely, weak and feeble. But you know what? God & my girl loves everyone, even the weak and feeble. I mark this entrance in my diary. It is important for me to realise that my girl loves me even if I have no clue what I'm talking about.

16. 11. 2019: I'm terribly bored today. This fuckin jail. And there's the smell...oh God. I feel like I want to vomit. Fuck this place. Nothing else to do but just sleep.

17. 11. 2019: This place sucks. Nothing else to do but just sleep.

18. 11. 2019: FUCK THIS PLACE

19. 11. 2019: Woke up today with a renewed obsession to finish my book by the time I get out of jail. I'll finish it at all cost and nothing... not even this ugly cell who is likely to compromise my beliefs, nothing will stop me. I will get writing done on a daily basis. Today I realised one thing...since I start writing this book it's more of a doomed relationship between me and the book and the more I write the more is about me. Sometimes the book kinda mirrors me like everything I

write actually happened in my life. Could this be me from the previous life? I have very much in common with the character. I wonder what my girl has to say about this. Could she have much in common with her character? Me & Julia have very much in common, that includes brushing our teeth in the same style and we both use manual brushes, I like black, she likes red. I like Colgate, she likes Weetabix. We also have same taste in music. But wait to see about our clothing obsession. She likes to dress in red, I like to wear black which means black and red in western culture are the two most sinister colours as red typically conveys the meaning of blood or anger and Julia definitely loves red because of this. She could be very angry at times especially with me. Wait and see. And black being my favourite colour, is that of darkness and that is me on writing. Being a very visually striking combination, both of these colours can also convey a sense of power and both, me & Julia very much favour for villainous which also explains the obsessive love for music me & Julia have in common. Unfortunately both of us are not a man nor a woman you can ally yourself with. Why? It's because I like Colgate and she likes Weetabix. I did said this in a previous brief. Some critics will suggest that all these statements are not true. I'm dying to see a reaction to the scenes coming out from this book. To be honest I want to get stopped in the street and I want people to point middle fingers at me and I want them to never leave me alone, because I know that once people will know everything it becomes like a game they all pretend they can play it. It might be better for all to become x-box characters. It is hard to find someone who understands all this that's because it is not me talking. It's my meds speaking. Oh god... one day I will look back at everything I wrote and get terribly embarrassed. No, of course I don't want you to think I'm depressed or that I want people to panic, those are just metaphors coming from my meds prescription. Gosh…one hour just passed and plenty of jail time to go. And there's also this smell. Yuck. My mental health will deteriorate so bad to the point I think about writing a new poem. I thought in the beginning this book will be a combination of poetry and photography but that didn't go very well. Let's see how I do on this poem.

Let's go!

Wev awe gotta common goal
That goal tay save souls
We can awe be superheroes
Twos upty awe da trolls
Wev only got diss life
Time to make a sacrifice
Let's hit da virus were it hurts
It act on good advice
Lets awe team up n unite
Time flies fast tonite
Lets raise well fir yerself
N the people special n yer life
Its scaped out red beams
On tha covid 19 spins
Gonna blast ye tay smithereens
Wer gonna shalter awe yer dreams

Gonna kill yer evil schemes
Yev messed way da wrong team
Its sirens out no retreat
Wer packen heat nat aw mean?
Wev won two world wars
So we know how its done
True brits know how its done
True grit ama true brit
Proud tay be ma nations son
Dis battles only just begun
Still wev got ye an da run
Soon tay be peter pan
No long till year spun
Saint Isaac on da run

20. 11. 2019: Feeling hopeless. Nothing to write. Uninspired and Incredibly bored. This place sucks.

21. 11. 2019: I'm so fuckin hungry and this bed is shit. The metal frame hurts my back. Fuck this place. Woke up in complete chaos style. There's just too many uncomfortable things around this cell that causes me distress. And that fuckin toilet smells so bad. There's a rather weird smell going out from it. The smell is persistent and smells like chlorine or ammonia or both. Something very bad. I feel like I'm in a gas chamber. One of those chambers from the Nazi's Germany of 1943. And who on earth would want a toilet

near his bed? Literally there's just one meter between my bed and the toilet. Are you fuckin kidding me? Only an alien will want that. I ain't a god damn alien. I'm a normal human being. That's just not right. I'm protesting for reforming toilets in jails. No one will give a shit anyway. Bastards-motherfuckers-jail-guards-getting-fat-on-spinning-chairs. I hope you all fart from spaghetti bolognese. On your spinning chairs of course. Shod be around 7:30 p.m and I can tell from the way the moon is positioned. Days gets shorter and my nights in jail gets longer. Haven't slept all night due to that ugly smell that comes from the toilet. Some fine intervals of moonlight getting inside my cell and this is good because it calms me down a little. The moon light and its energy it generates space weather in my cell but minutes later started to rain. Typical Scotish weather. An experience? Yeah right. For some is fine. For some is an unremarkable hell. Taking a good look out the window to see what's all about. First thing I see is the sea. It looks like a blanket. The sea it seems calmer tonight. This is the first time I am patient to explore the surroundings of this jail. To be honest I have a good view from my window. I don't even know where in the hell I am. Probably in hell. All hells are the same but this one is a rather quiet hell set on a island. Looking west I see more sea. Looking east plenty more sea. Definitely on a island. I mark this entrance in my diary so I know I am on a island in case I forget where I am. And there's also the fear that I might be used for laboratory experiments then left in this cell with no memory to know who I am. That will be terrifying. All sort of shit can happen in jail especially in a weirdos place. Pretty much the place where I'm now. There's a car park not too far from my building. A woman wearing a white uniform is smoking and she looks more like a doctor or a nurse. A man is joining her company. He lit up his ciggy. Can this be what I think it is? Actually I tell you what happened. The fucker just touched her cunt and seconds later is sucking her tits. What the fuck? Yes, behind the jail wall two horny employees hit back on their genitals. "I hope you both fart from spaghetti bolognese…you motherfuckers." I hope they heard me. Came back into my bed and start crying. Went out from the bed to check the moon. It's glowing. No sign of these two. They probably thought I'm just another weirdo on existential crisis. Went back to bed trying to calm down and I nearly felt asleep when suddenly I hear the cell door getting open. A prison officer brings me a meal saying that I shod eat and get some sleep. Half bread, huge slice of fried sausage, can of beans, pack of biscuits and a nice cup of tea. Life is now worth living. I eat almost half the food in ten seconds and gave thanks to God. Absolutely everything happened to me now it makes my night. I thank the officer and gave him a smile. I mark this entrance in my diary. It is important for me to monitor my eating habits.

22. 11. 2019: How are you today? I'm fine thanks in jail! How was your day at work? Do you know any songs? Do you like cats? Do you prefer the city or the country? I don't prefer the jail. Apparently has become the ultimate creative place to write a book about my fine self. A wonderful addition to the canon of generic house of writers that is just so ideal to read at an acceptable low light or in a trendy bar where real estate moguls congregate to discuss housing prices, eat deconstructed pulled pork sandwiches that cost twenty three

pounds each and plays future club anthems. For what I call an ideal place. Just received my jail food and it literally scared me. Bowl of soup which looked just like alien blood. Some green texture with large lumps of powder. Yuck. Gosh...I need a way out from this negative mindset and turn back to reality, hit a few good sentences and the rest will follow. I need to write. I need to sleep. I need to eat. Eventually I'll survive this shit.

23. 11. 2019: Am I in a crazy people's place writing crazy things coming from a crazy mind? Or I'm in my worst nightmare! Seriously. I swear everything I write here is real jail life happening around the clock. Dreadful weather outside. Violent wind. Roaring sea. It seems to be normal Scotish weather. Shetland weather. Island weather. In the middle of the sea weather. Some sort of weather I never seen in my entire life. Makes you wonder why my writing changes like the weather. Perhaps the weather itself plays an influential role in my writing. There's one ugly bug on the floor. By the way, the floor is made of stone. More like a timeless and highly durable stoned floor. Typical jail floor. Although, I would prefer a marble style. It would be an excellent choice to make my 100 days in jail an ambience of both, luxury and antiquity. It will blend well with my character. This Saint Isaac character is a beautiful natural grain and likes a handsome porous stone on my floor. Wait, the bug is making a move. He must be hungry. It's black and has long legs. Has teeny tiny eyes so he can hide under my bed. I bet this fucker can't wait for me to go back to sleep so he can bite a chunk of meat from me. Skinny black legs so he can climb on my back. Horrible hairy back so he can

transform himself into a bat. Big boogy eyes so he can watch me in the dark. Warning! There's an alien in my cell. I think is looking for a tasty snack. I might eat you before you eat me you horrible alien bug. This story might put me into a glossy spot lamination on the paperback cover of a fancy magazine. "A funny, clever storyteller by the name of Saint Isaac, starving himself in jail but happy with eating hairy bugs." Breaking news! Wait, the bug just spoke to me... it says it will open my cell door in 100 days or less if I'm going to be a good boy on the outside, stop taking drugs, get a normal job and eventually settle down and get myself a wife. "Sure, i'll do any of that." And furiously smashed the bug with my right foot. I fuckin hate being here. I hate this place. Fuck this place. I'm going to bed. Nothing else to do. Fuck off.

24. 11. 2019: The weather is the same. The jail is the same. My cell is the same. I am the same. My writing is the same. My life is the same. My thoughts are the same. The floor is not the same. For my own safety I had to put a blanket in the window so I can stop the rain keep coming in. The wind blows water in my cell. I have a wet floor. Cant' be any more worse than this. Earlier today I been visited by a prison guard to bring me a new treatment. I refused. He insisted I shod swallow three weird looking pills. One yellow, one blue and one red saying if I swallow them everything will be alright and I enter wonderland. He also mention something about going down the rabbit hole. I don't even know what means. I told him to fuck off. Obviously he left immediately. Don't mess with crazy people. I'm not crazy. I just look that way. For the sake of this book. Gone are the days where

crazy is much of a threat anymore. People seem to think dealing with a crazy person has become the norm. When someone gets that look in their eyes, you are supposed to run. Now, finding someone who seems calm, quiet and peaceful is actually a bigger threat. Being institutionalised isn't really that terrifying. It can be like a resort. But where I am now is not even closer to that. An island to reset to zero? Is this the thing I sign up? Where in the hell is that place? Have I not been nice enough with people? Why put away in such a horrible place? Well...wait to see what happens next. I will escape in an imaginary world where I can make fun of tyrants, laugh at their behaviour, fart in their face, shit on their porcelain white fake teeth, eat, drink, fuck, take drugs and be merry, and take back that creative freedom I been stripped off, and I will take this fight by using nothing but just pen and pepper. Don't worry, I'm not crazy. I just look that way so I can write more compelling stories. Writers perform these actions along a plot line so the readers can be the driving force behind great stories and writers know that readers are the driving force behind their stories. Although, it seems to me that most writers are so involved in the technical bullshit, you know, the stuff that crafts the manuscript, to the point they forgot the elements that interest readers. Readers come to fiction to find something they can't get in their daily lives. Just as pilots can practise flying without leaving the ground, people who read fiction lose themselves inside the world of a fictional character while reading a story, and believe it or not you may actually end up changing your own behaviour and thoughts to match that of the character, as if they were your own. Experience-taking, each time they open a novel. Show them you've got a world for them to explore, characters to root for, plot that will

entice them, and they will give you all their time to read on. So…
come to fiction to find something you can't get in your daily lives.
The wind blows so much water in my cell. I have to find a way to get
it sorted otherwise I end up with more than just a wet floor. More like
an ocean on the jail floor. And I can't even swim.

25. 11. 2019: Good morning. How are you today? Because I don't
feel okay. Earlier I had a visit from the prison governor and was
more than kind from him to tell me that this place is not such a bad
place after all and I shod get used to it otherwise he will increase my
days in jail. But rest assured my stay it will be comfortable until I
finish the book. I don't feel too comfortable here. He told me to smile,
I told him to fuck off from my cell. He eventually did left the cell. I'm
seventeen days in jail out of one hundred. What's that…83 more to
go? For fuck sake, just too many. This ain't good at all. Right now
all I can do is sleep all day, write short stories in the night time, shit,
eat the jail food, not masturbate because is bad for the health, and
eventually repeat the whole thing. And some prayer in between
thinking God is here to offer me some form of help. The sea is
calmer. Some birds flying near my window. A rare and irregular
visitor approaches my window. It looks like a spotted woodpecker.
It's black and with some white plumage and a red patch on the lower
belly. Beautiful bird. If is a real woodpecker bird then can fuck off. I
once heard a story about these small motherfuckers that are a bad
sign. Fuck off from my window you small alien unless you

want me to eat you alive. Gosh...I feel intensified when I think of my 83 days in jail. Yes, I'm counting. I thought about getting out from this cell for some exercise. I could do with some fresh air. I mean, common, is been seventeen days locked inside this ugly cell. I feel terribly depressed in this cubicle would love to get out for some exercise. Ten minutes waiting on the door after a few shouts and no sign of humans on this wing. Myself with myself. Bastards, I hope they fart from spaghetti bolognese. Off to bed. What else can I do but just sleep. Sleep in the day time. Sleep in the night time. Some writing now and then. Repeat. Such a fucked-up life in jail.

26. 11. 2019: A prison taint is on everything in my cell. Ugly rusty walls with traces of bad smell...ammonia or something. Yuck. Ugly stuff from years of confinement. I can imagine dozens of men kept captive in this cell for the past few decades. Lurking their sins in this cell. Just found out this prison was built in early 1800's Victorian time. Think about that. Think about how many men went in and out this cell. Too many. It probably makes sense the "death-like-smell" all over this place. The imprisoned air. The imprisoned light. The imprisoned damp. The imprisoned man. Sadly, that will be me. This confinement is slowly becoming a problem for my writing. I'm starting to lack plot in my story. And my story had better deliver otherwise I'll get murdered in comments. God help my tweeter feed. I better come up with something fresh, a new story or something so I can make the next 200 pages worth reading. I actually don't know if I'm planing to write 300 pages. When day 100 hits I close the book for good. At some point it may lead to another book. Another book for a lucky penny. You know what? Fuck this bed...it's all rusty iron, bad-motherfucker-ugly-smelly-bed. Full of bed bugs. Fuck this place. This jail is a joke. There's bites all over my body. The table I write is rotten wood gone dump and this makes my writing go mad. And there's also a sensation of gassed air... is all faint and it makes me feel weak and dizzy and sometimes close to losing consciousness. I sometimes run to the window and take a deep breath of fresh air to calm my thoughts. There's also a huge lamp in the upper corner of the cell that makes me mad. At-all-time-light. They keep it this way so they can keep an eye on me in case I attempt to wash my hands. Whatever. Like it really matters. I'm already dirty as a black rock found on the bottom of a pile of crap. This cell is disgusting.

Everything feels like a tomb but rather a vault with no way out. The air I breathe is so polluted that it makes my writing go mad. Please someone keep an open mind that soon I'll become a recovered angry man. By the way there's a letter just came in and is addressed to me. It's been slipped under the door by a prison guard. It says is from the governor and I'm being instructed to get ready at exact 11:00 a.m tomorrow for I'm about to get some fresh air. One full hour in the exercise yard just for me. But I ain't have a watch in jail. I'll just stay all day in front of the door until someone will eventually open it for me. Wanna get out.

26. 11. 2019: My nineteen day in jail it feels more like my eighteen birthday in hell. I feel exactly the same. To let you know, only illustrations I remember from my eighteen birthday, more like small ones at the beginning of each chapter. I believe this one is definitely my eighteen birthday chapter. It was my birthday and with the money I got from my parents, which was around 200 euros, I went to the prostitutes. I paid the puta all my money and I told her to rock my cock off but to do it like in the cowboy movies. Especially the rowdy Old Western style. Or like in Billy the Kid, Buffalo Bill and Rio Bravo. These were my favourite styles. I told the puta if she can do these styles. The puta said yes of course. So, with all that said the puta told me to go into a special room and stay there until she's getting prepared. She also told me that she's going to wear the Buffalo Bill hat. I was so excited. I took out my cock and start doing the rodeo by myself. I wanted to show this puta my skill at riding broncos. You know...first ever sex, losing my virginity, I wanted to make it special.

By the way, the real Saint Isaac was a wild bison hunter and snowman. Now here's the bad news. I didn't knew that when I gave my money I give it to the chief puta in charge of the bookings, and she was not the puta I supposed to hang around with. She was more like a receptionist. I admit…the puta in front of house was a splendid beauty. Ten minutes later a middle-aged woman who just wanted a companion for the evening entered the room I was waiting. Here I

was looking at an old bag around the age of 60. "Are you the young man who came in my rural brothel?" The puta asked. She barely spoke but she did told me that she is indeed the puta I supposed to shag. "Let me give you a regular"— the puta said. I had no idea what on earth is a regular. I could tell she had been drinking. We're sitting on the bed and I'm trying to ask her…"Who are you." or…"Give me my money back." I kept the mood light and friendly. I could be her grandson that old she was. Only to begin taking her clothes off, panties, bra, I saw a big cock. The puta was a trans-woman. And her cock was also bigger than mine. I stand up and within a second I wanted to kill myself. God damn puta. It messed up my eighteen birthday. A few days later I was passing by the brothel but not to look for another puta but just randomly passing by on my way home and one of the putas recognised me immediately. She told me to come by for a regular. I told her to fuck off. From the distance she shouted at me and said that her friend told her she wished I was her best friend. Yeah right….and I showed her my middle finger. I ain't getting fucked by a hard punch of sentiments. I think is time for me to get some fresh air. Finally. It's time for me to take my turtle for a walk in the jail court yard. Life is worth living. It took me a minute to get around my cell and find the only piece of clothing I have to wear. My orange striped pyjamas. Also my jail uniform. At last, now I look like a proper prisoner. At last. My instructions given to me by the chief governor were to look like a regular prisoner. He also told me to intentionally make my pants look ripped so I can look like the others. You know...a weirdo. Unstable. Apparently this was the only way to blend in with the others and look like them so I can be left alone. I supposed to look like the others who frequented the jail. This was the only way to not get into any troubles with the big guys. You don't mess with the crazy but I'm also a little crazy who haven't even heard the word crazy. It's a crazy thing to make it look crazy. For the day I was no longer Saint Isaac, instead, I was prisoner '1-800-DIAL-A-COOKIE-NOW' from cell number 13. Upon getting out the cell my hands were pulled back and handcuffed with half-way-chewed-bubble-gum just in case I try to escape the jail yard. I picked up my dull looking shoes and I haven't even thought of shining them and as I entered the corridor I frowned into the mirror but it was a reflection from a broken window. Not sure if it was me. If indeed was me I couldn't recognise myself. I looked rather weird. Face looking incredibly dull. Huge beard and terrible eye bags. Also dirt all over the face. There were also cracks in my skin's surface giving me the appearance of a middle age man. And I'm only thirty. I think I start hate mirrors. But I could also imagine myself like an elder genius who wrote a book on literary madness. I think I prefer that way. The fuckin bed bugs made me look that way. They sucked all my life from me. I have found out that bed bugs open themselves to my wise blood and they stick and suck my spirit and they do it contemplatively as often as they feel until they feel re-energised and they may even experience a surge of creativity hence you shod definitely continue reading. You may as well experience wise blood too from my writing. "Do you have any injuries I should know?" The chief governor asked me. Yes, plenty of bed bugs bites and I have them all over my body and a lack of blood in the whole of my heart." "You'll be fine" — The chief governor said. "Okay, move out" —

Yes chief. As I exited the building and entered the exercise yard and by the way this yard is more of a piece of enclosed ground at the back entrance of the jail. This ground looks totally different from the other wing. I couldn't stop thinking about how amazing is to enjoy a deep breath of fresh air. I really enjoy that. I'm alive. As I breathe deeply the fresh air coming in through my nose fully nourished my lungs and I will notice that I was getting better from each breath of fresh air I take in. The cell and its imprisoned smell nearly killed me. In the exercise yard and I successful passed the bell boys which is a jail-slang used for glamorous psychopaths. Wait a second...I think I already recognise one. I swear I seen him on TV. It's Jack the pigeon ripper who killed pigeon meatballs with tomato sauce. He was on the run with the pigeon trolley and here he is now in jail done for pigeon meatballs. Motherfucker. He deserves to root in jail. God damn it...I'm surrounded by psychopaths. Why do I constantly feel like I need to take a deep breath and get the fuck out from this place. Concealing myself from the rest of the nuts is a good bet. Don't forget I am myself pretending to be a nut. When I arrived here two weeks ago the jail was very loud with hundreds of prisoners shouting all over the place. I'm wondering where in the hell are all of them? In hell of course. This place is one of the most confusing things about life and is rather hard for me to explain. It is difficult for confused newcomers like me. Gosh I need a bath, nice bed facing big TV, glass of wine, plenty of cake and a massage on my feet. Taking a note of this. It is important for me to know what I need when I get out of jail. I'm in D wing and this is a different jail building. It's light and airy here, almost like a well-regulated fancy motel. Oh my...you not gonna believe this...someone actually wrote at the entrance of the building "Crispy Bacon Motel." It's on a wooden board and is hanged just above the door. It appears this wing is for well behaved prisoners. Definitely not me. In C wing right now and this is the jail I stayed for only a couple of days. Here you get to see the whole gamut of insanity. Some of the prisoners here are violently insane and even dangerous, but they are locked-in. Some of them scream but you soon become accustomed to that. Some talk incessantly often choosing nighttime for their loudest tirades. The rules are less strict in my wing than in C wing. By the way I'm in A wing. A jail building reserved only for literary talents. It happens to be reserved only for me. The down side in my wing is that is an observation wing, the patient, or prisoner, is allowed a good deal of rope to hang himself. Just in case things don't turn out well or how the prisoner hoped to be. I'm passing C wing and cells seems very small even smaller than mine but very clean and tidy, which is strange because this wing is hell. It accommodates all types of dangerous characters. Psychopaths especially. This is also where Jack the pigeon ripper lives. The windows seems to be barred. I am being walked back to my cell and I wouldn't go out from it again until my term is done. I'm Terrified, mortified, petrified...stupefied by this fuckin ugly jail. As they said...it would be done soon. I went to bed thinking greatly discouraged how life can be in a weirdos jail. Lying in bed and quite bitterly unhappy that this should never happen to me. Being in jail. I'm kinda accusing myself, which might be the major element in my condition. If I had been worked my ass hard, all this shit could be avoided. God damn it. An awful mess of things will never exist in my life if only chose the rightful path in life, be a good boy, work hard and stay with my creative life. I mark this entrance in my diary. It is important for me to take notes of anything hopeful. I just want to go to sleep in the hope to remove this irritation from me.

27. 11. 2019: I think I have much to say about everything I dreamed last night. My last night dream was so cool. Short story — it was a dream that happened in real life. Long story — it was a dream where I housed all my apples and chocolates which I love so much. Very long story — it was a dream where I will be tomorrow. You see...the only way to survive this hell and make a life where I am free to do what I want, when I want, and with who I want is when I dream. That's the only way it will be a tomorrow for me. Today I'm in jail. Tomorrow I'm not free. But when I dream I am indeed. Very. Much. Free. Right now I think I have much to say about my dream. In my dream I was free from the prison discipline. But trapped in a story of a fated love triangle. And guess who made my night long and humid? This has to be my girl.

Dear Julia,

My girl...I'm so in love with you...ai ai ai...I'm so in love with you. Please don't think like..."Oh, another story, he never stops." Yes my girl, another story. Men tell stories. Women get on with it. I don't expect from you a parade, nor a medal or a mentioning on your insta feed. Simply pick up the pieces and start puzzling because this is a gut-punch in the mystery and thriller category. No wonder it helped the author beat any conversation in a written script. Life is a strange game at least once every five pages in "Blood And Guts In Jail." Listen girl...on the night before last night I made a wow to myself to tell the truth that often lies because "I'm Very Into You." And since in jail I have become even more into you. Let me start with last night, because It was a cold and clear night last night and the stars were twinkling brightly above my jail bed. Around midnight I decided to go to sleep. Suddenly I start to dream. You were in my dream. The dream was so cool...I saw the jail gates open in my dream. For some reason the jail gates were made out of apples and chocolates which I love so much. Finally, I was free from the prison discipline. Life on the inside, my-ups-and-downs kinda made me hate prison discipline. It kinda marked my life but marked the hard way. You know...like the iron that leaves a brown mark on the sleeve. Damn it. The fine art of ironing is not my thing. The heartbreaking true story was that I had nowhere to go. I was homeless. Penniless. Still, I was wearing my best set of clothing. White shirt, black trousers, red bowtie, pair of Chelseas, and a nice brownish blazer. Looking more like a Wall Street geza. By the way...a geza is typically a funny, intelligent, lovable person. More like me. As I was saying...Yes, I was telling you about my clothing. Actually...these were the exact clothing I left home for jail. I must also tell you that these were my only clothing. The only clothing I once had at home. Well...more like an...ex-home. Bad news from my landlord. He decided to evict me. And he evicted me with all I had...my vinyl record collection and everything else in between, recording studio included. You know... the stuff I lived and breathe for...for my entire life...my creative life. Kinda makes me cry. It's okay to cry. I never thought I'd see myself cry. Just so you know...it hurts but it's all on me. Let my wipe my tears. With the horrific events of my past I was now walking free chasing the road of freedom. Determined to never touch drugs again. Determined to return to my creative life. In a way...you reminded me of who I prefer to be. Still in a dream. But now I imagine where I shod head first. I think it was around midnight when I arrived in Glasgow central station. I preferred the buss station. It was so cool to see people walking freely around. I was too walking freely. 100 days trapped in a two meter cubicle kinda messed up my eulerian destiny. Couldn't believe I was walking free. And in the middle of the night... "Walking In The Night." Strange, isn't it? Because if you google this short sentence it kinda reveals my favourite piece of art in the context of four minutes and twelve seconds audio. I move further and there were a bunch of teenagers riding skateboards in the middle of the night. Can you believe that? Others were ridding BMX bicycles. The cool thing was I was riding on my freedom more than ever. Nothing was taken for granted. By this time it was nearly 2:00 a.m. By the way...finally I seen the freaking time. Can you believe for 100 days I haven't seen time! I mean, time is all around us, in any shape, form or style. Babylonians and Egyptians invented time 5000 years ago. Did you knew that? By the way...there were a bunch of people eating nice food not too far from me. Oh Gosh it smelled so good. Cooked food I think it was. Something nice like a good quality pizza. But a few of them also had a bunch of hamburgers. Some McDonalds bags too. I kept looking at them for quite some time. A couple of guys looked back at me and I felt rather embarrassed...I don't know how shod I put it but I think one of them actually spot me and it was more like..."is he hungry or...what's wrong with him?" Kinda like that. Kinda like that...was me. Precisely me. I let them be so I came back in my caravan of dreams. Most important I was free. Yes, I was telling you about time. I was watching the bus station clock. Huge round clock. In a way it caused me great enthusiasm to keep watch it. I think I stared at that god damn clock for longer than an hour. In jail I was staring at white walls. Now, free, I was starting at anything. Anything was taken not for granted. Still, very hungry. In my pocket I had absolutely nothing. In my stomach I was having a lion and a tiger as my pets and they were too asking for food. I decided to take my pets for a walk in the nearby park. I think it was around 4.00 a.m by now…sitting alone in the nearest park. While I was there I saw a light at the end of the park. The park was mostly dark. No lights at all on the aisle. In front of me there was a passage that lead to a building and it looked more like a church or theatre…I don't know exactly. It was dark. On my right side it was the bus station. Some aircraft passing above my head. But I guess aircrafts must pass above heads. Glasgow airport was just a couple of miles away. My focus was that light at the end of the park. I walked by slowly and went inside the light. I could actually walk inside the light which was strange. When I got inside suddenly there was a big darkness. The light disappeared. Still…a little bit of light from the moonlight. By the way…the moonlight reminds me of my nights in jail. I think those nights were my only…okay nights…also my lamp above my jail bed. I'm flipping past tense and present tense like I can't stop thinking how hungry I am. Sorry. Life can be strange in "Blood And Guts In Jail." Either way my girl, this story is one that you'll never forget. Not even if you had a wild night with me in bed. I hope you don't take this the wrong way. Was that a teardrop in your eye? Let me take a seat my girl. It's nice and dark out here. By the way I could do with a cigarette. You have a spare one? It's okay, I'll ask you next time. I promise I'll ask you next time. Next time we see each-other the first thing I will say to you is…"You have a spare cigarette." Why? In this way you'll remember my "Blood And Guts In Jail." By the way…the light is back. This time is the odd aisle lighting. Still...it's strange how the light came instantly just when I was talking to you. It's like you been listening to me. Otherwise It turns out I was hallucinating. In my dreams I randomly hallucinate. Sometimes I have this strange feeling that you're trying to communicate with me in a way or another... something like... I'm very into you. Do you? I do. Again, I'm flipping past tense and present tense like I can't stop thinking about you. Maybe is because I have a crush on you. Do you? I do. Listen girl, me and you are the same if not fragments of the same song we both listen on the radio. The kind of song with a nervous breakdown. It's a good song. With that kind of song you hit every abandoned heart including my soul. How incredible. A song can literally make you see episodes from your past. I was shocked to find out they didn't approve the CD I requested with my favourite songs. Life in jail can be strange without my favourite songs. But what could I say? One day I'll get out and play my favourite Spotify playlist. Probably a smooth radio too. Listen girl, we know each-others so little since I got the jail but we talk about one another so much. So much that I'm very into you. Do you? I do. Still got that glint in your eye? It makes me feel like I don't ever wanna say goodbye. Nearly 5:00 a.m. and is time for me to wake up and go back to my jail bed. Emotions taking over because I want to spend more time here with you. Oh god damn it... I'm not being good at this at all. Such are the delights of talking in your dreams.

28. 11. 2019: Woke up piling in my head a smooth radio mix I had last night and by the way last night I had the coolest ever dream. At least the best dream I had since long ago. It turns out It was indeed just a dream. Back to jail life...oh gosh I actually lost the count of my jail days. Shod be somewhere around 20 days in. If that's the correct number then 80 more to go until I'm out. Just too many. Way too many. But let's look on the bright side. Imagine the amount of piles of stories I can write for the next 80 days. Piles of stories. Read on and I tell you everything. There's a line of dialogue for everything in "Blood And Guts In Jail." Gosh...I so much want a peach ice cream with a brownie sundae on top. It will help me forget the dream I had last night. I'd come along way to think about this dream I had last night. I'm telling you when you say words that somehow causes emotion-like-signs... stuff like enjoyment, sadness, fear, some anger and surprise, admiration and adoration are risk factors for what happens next. To be honest with you I just don't want to cause emotional distress for absolutely no one including me. What I said last night can relate to many. Just as the music you love tells you who you are, and by the way, music does accurately tells you who you are because you love your favourite song in such a way that is associated with an intense emotional experience in your life. It can affect someone in an emotional way for the rest of their life. I'm again a melanotic fool and I keep come back to these moments of madness to feed my story which also happens to feed my book. I tried to hit the nail but instead I hit my thumb.

29. 11. 2019: One could get addicted to this line of work that's why today I can't write anything. In bed keep holding of my teddy bear. My jail food have put me off script for a day of sleep. One could get addicted to this type of sleep. Tomorrow I will try create some beautiful sentences and spin a stunning metaphor between my pages. If not I'll use the language of imagery, craft a dialogue about some gorgeous descriptions about my looks and tell you how beautiful I am because these days I am very beautiful. Exquisite, fire-breathing looks. Full of passion, regret and longing desire for a portion of Victoria sponge cake. Fuck this jail food. It sucks.

30. 11. 2019: Oh my jail days for I am as lonely as a morning soundtrack on a Russian radio. I knew once a song played on a Russian radio and it was about some intense affairs with my life and just to let you know that my life is thwarted by misunderstanding after misunderstanding, typically because of guilt or a belief that discovery would lead to trouble, that's why I prefer to stick with secretive and often fictional stories, attempting to avoid notice from my real past. If you want I can give you plenty of fictional themes and obsessions about my past. One of them is Jackfruits with a blow of Spotify playlist. And I prefer a techno playlist. That's exactly where I want to be right now, between my playlists, listening a blend of techno-pop also termed synth-pop or electro-pop, and in the same time holding a ripen banana in my right hand...thinking how the world ends... I do this when days are long and humid. Another obsession is to do whatever I like. But that may be a rule for life as well for my writing. Sometimes I think of my writing as part of the

fictional universe of Saint Isaac franchise. You buy Saint Isaac's ticket, it takes you on a ride through bosky, dimly related hinterlands until you scream loud: "I'm a Normal Human Being, Get Me The Fuck Out Of Here." The fortune teller told me all about this. He's my local priest.

1. 2. 2019: Earlier today I was given a pile of plain white paper by the prison governor. It was addressed to my name and my name written in capitals: SAINT ISAAC. But there was also a small note attached to an envelope. It says: keep writing. I was actually impressed by this small gesture from the governor. It made a difference to my day. He then left the cell. Upon leaving he wag his tail which was more of a cute way of him to say that he will like some royalties added to his belt. It seems he really pushes his financial plans with me. By the way..I only found out he is a retired insurance salesmen. Which makes perfectly sense why he's trialing his belt and suspenders on me. I also noticed something else on him and my conspiracies lays in the practiced accent of his shyness. I bet if I organise a row of tickles on him I won't be surprised how fluent he can speak Russian language but with a practiced accent that could probably fool any Intelligence officer. I'm telling you...I'm being watched by a barn owl. Wait, there's another note from him...I just found it in the pile of paper. By the way...good looking paper. Nice and soft. I actually like it. The second note says that he will like only one point. A "point"was an industry standard slang that means for every book sold he would get 1% of the royalties earned. In the book sales industry points are what everyone is looking for that

includes the prison governor. And if my book sales really takes off there's no limit to the amount the governor can make. This sounds to me more of a deal. Although looking at the way he left the cell I was struck by how much he resembled a cute way a dog would tell us they're happy and moving their tail to get a better picture of their body language. Motherfucker. Well...he got what he want. I got a huge pile of paper to keep up with my writing. Time to go full potatoes. Waging my tail. Howl. Howl.

2. 12. 2019: I just looked in the mirror for the first time in one month...I look diminished with a weak heart. If I write anything it will make my writing sound so mad. For today is better to not be the subject of a conversation. The ancient Greeks will agree with me.

3. 12. 2019: This really upset me. I asked the prison guard if there are any letters for me and he said there isn't any. I'm thinking to write a second letter to my girl. And I'll do it in a song style. I'll also give this song a name...Weetabix. Once I named one of my songs, Weetabix. It's a nice chill out four-on-the floor version that helps with a comfortable walking to the breakfast table. Anything to make my girl write me a letter. I'll do anything. I'll even try to upset her to get some attention going.

Dear Julia,

There's something I must tell you. If we can't be together then perhaps we can be friends? Disagreement is something normal. I understand if you don't like me anymore. Listen girl...for years I liked you and I liked you like my morning breakfast roll. And by the way these days I prefer a bacon roll. But in the same time for the past six months I also cheated on you and I done it with an Iceland girl. Her name is Hekla and she owns the best exotic Marigold hotel in Iceland. Tough girl, smart and powerful. I believe these are some of the traits I like about her. After six months we broke up. Well...it wasn't really anything going but just an online fling. She liked one of my tweets. I gave it a retweet and...pretty much thats it. I just thought I can tell you now. Since I got the jail I became a man of God and God told me last night to confess my sins against you. Did that hurt you? Is it okay to forgive me? You told me once if I ever cheat on you and I tell you all about you'll immediately forgive me. Can you now give me the big smile? I give you mine. If that's still not okay then let me be your enemy so I can coexist. I'd always prefer to be friends with someone when angry with me but if they're not interested then I consider being enemies the next best option. Why? Because if you hate me you're more likely to talk with me. Listen girl...I love you and I'm so much into you and I'm sure you're pretty much the same with me. If you feel passionate about me in a negative way at some point you'll probably say to your friends... "God damn it I can't stand my man for he is in jail and he also cheated on me." Your friends is going to ask you..."Why?"... and just like that I've become the subject of a conversation then we will be back together again. But if we can't get that I'll take the hate but I'll still love you. You know I love you. I'm sorry you had to hear this. Really, I'm sorry. However, let's feel good. The ancients Greeks will agree with me. I miss my girl. Signed, Saint Isaac.

4. 12. 2019: Woke up with the prison officer on my bed handling me a letter. It appears the letter I sent yesterday went out as an e-mail. They scan what I wrote and sent it to the recipient by electronic transfer. Which means my girl already got in touch with the jail and provided her contact details. She's definitely into me. I can't wait to open my letter. Must be some wonderful news. Let me see what it says…

"Listen…Shut ye geggie! Yer aff yer heid? Ya doaty donkey! Shut yer pus and dunt write me again! I won't fuk with ya anymore cus you like the one from Iceland. Fuck off!

5. 12. 2019: Yesterday went straight to bed for I was terribly upset from the news received from Julia. I won't even talk about it. Well… she went full potatoes on me. Whatever. Bipolar wee little pus. You know what? I actually lost the count of my days in jail. A large capacity of jail time is still to go. I wont even count any days for it's depressing. Very little food I had today. I hate jail food. I'll be a stick and a half when I get out. Staying alive is what matters right now. One thing I noticed recently is my writing. I have become a better writer. The more I write the more makes me think because thinking teaches you critical thinking. It takes practice and I'm already practicing my skill in jail. By the time I get out I might even graduate as a skilled writer. Not sure about my behaviour but there's still time to get things right, that includes my mental health for at times it can be all over the place. And I can tell you there's not enough place in my cell for my mental health to get well. Oh my jails days…I really don't know what to write next. This cell is killing me. It's hard to write something from literally nowhere. There's no inspiration here. Nothing to feed my mind. All I see is a white wall in front of me. I might start hating colour white for the rest of my life. I'm craving for some clear blue skies of logic and reason and this cell is not just clouding my writing but it's also clouding my judgement. And when I get upset I go chaos style…jail effect all over me. Oh my gosh…I hear crackle noise in the background and it's killing me. When I desire a pinch of silence this cell crackle away in the background. It's like the sound from an old Russian radio. Does bad to my creative mind. It creates excessive thinking. The excessive thinking is more like the internal chatter of a monkey. It never stops. It always has something to say…spreading worse than Covid-19 virus and it's spreading in a

quite simple desperate human way. Too truly...I don't even know where I'm going with my writing. I'll just keep everything for a brilliant moment of laughter. I was just thinking... do you you think my writing will ever be considered a stellar production, visionary, or some kind of reference of life in jail? As you can see I kinda rebel against the narrow, normative society and few other personal things in between and I do it by being both, an absolute triumph and absolute asshole. Could this be because I'm a writer trapped in a prisoner's world? Would someone ever believe this nonsense that is slowly making sense...I did not even researched very well the character. Everything is on autopilot and is spreading worse than a virus. Let me mark this in my diary. It is important for me to try stay away from this virus. I do have a jail diary. The reality is often this jail diary is not real. Most of its pages are artefacts of the mind. For now all I can do is put brilliant thoughts into text and text into paper and to do it more often than I realise...until I realise where everything comes from...from a prisoner's mind. It could be. For now I shod consider some fairly happy sleep, obviously much exhausted by my clever thinking.

6. 12. 2019: I feel like shit. I am high on jail food, cold tea, bed bugs, and of course...plenty of Julia...pilling in my thoughts. This time she entered in all my thoughts and I can barely get rid of her. If I don't write her again I might never do it again. I must write her again. It might be the last time I write her again unless she makes me write her again. Again...I love her. Or it's the jail effect making a mark on me. It could be. If that's the case pray for me I'll still be alive. Do it

with candles, cigarettes, scramble eggs, your relaxing music mix, even macaroni cheese if that is your thing. Pray for me I will not be dumped by my glorified sexy girl. I have this feeling in my gut that soon I will be entering a chain of letters. And I always trust my gut. My gut never lies to me. It's time for a new adventure, full of passion, regret and longing and stories of a fated love triangle. Now the new landmark of my writing for the next few pages. It's funny because until I landed in jail I didn't even knew how to write a letter. But not just no idea about writing a normal letter but also absolutely no idea about love letters. I mean...common a love letter? I must be a power-man if I can do all this. But it is not me who's doing the writing but Writer Isaac Bjorn who's doing the typing. I'm just dictating in a quite desperate human way. Too truly...I don't even know where I'm going with this writing. I better do it in a "e-mail a prisoner" style. Jail cable.

..e-mail a prisoner. Copy...saint Isaac, cell 13

Dear Julia,

Being attracted to bad guys is one thing. Living with one is a completely different story. In a few weeks I'm out of jail and I thought I could ask to live with you at least for a while. I know this is not at all new to you but you're the only one I put my hope into. Did I just put a smile on your face? I know I did. By the way...I love your smile, so soft and gentle. It's sexy. I also know you like the word sexy. That's because you are sexy. Listen girl...first of all the reason I'm writing to you is because I'm very into you and I just can't stop thinking about you. You are everything what's missing from me. You complete me. Did I told you how beautiful you are? You're tall, slender and breathtaking gorgeous girl. When I think of you it's love at first triangle. I can even do it with closed eyes. Right now I'm imagining a triangle. Is that you? I now imagine I catch your eyes and you'll look at me with a smile. When you do that it's absolutely love at first sight. You'll be amazed to know how good you look in your favourite red dress, black high heals and holding a book in your right hand. You are so beautiful girl. I'm just into my first month of my jail sentence and all I do is cry all day because I miss you. When I go to sleep the tears don't stop. And you know why? Because I miss you. God damn it...I talked too much and you been always a good listener. That's because you always knew I'm going to say something stupid. I now become stupid. Wise people always say less than necessary. Stupid people always speaks too much. I thought I praise you and in return I will receive some approval or admiration from you. Somehow I managed to dig my own hole around you. Can I take you for a coffee when I get out? We go down south and stay at your favourite five star. You like Ritz? I thought like Weetabix. Anything you want. I will get you a full box of cereals. It's all on me. I still have a couple of Bitcoin in my saving account. I'll take it all out and splash on you. It will be a nice affair for both of us. A fantastic affair for both of us. Wait, someone just open my cell. Jail food just came in. I'll use this opportunity to handle my letter. Cable me softly. I love you girl. Yours thru beans on toast, Saint Isaac

P.S, a bunch of people wrote me the other day. They all ask me these questions..."Please tell us who is this heroine of yours, tell us about this angel…does she flies? What about the colours of her socks? Is she wearing red or black? Perhaps white? Does she likes coffee or carrot juice? What about food…She likes her steak rare? Well done or medium well? Salty? With French fries on the side? What about bread? White or brown? We want to know who she is." I told them that I can't do that. I told them you will get very upset. I told them you prefer to remain a mystery in the fiction & romance category. That includes the way you like your steak. Write me anything. I love ya.

7. 12. 2019 ..e-mail a prisoner. Copy…Julia to cell 13

Listen, Shut ye geggie! Yer aff yer heid ya doaty dobber! Fuck off!
Ya tell anything I'll ride ya in tae battle with ma wee wand! Bolt ya
rocket or I bile yer heid with tha butcher's Lorne sausage. Ya fuckin
pocket monkey. Fuck off. Ah'll ragdoll ye if Ai get ye!

8. 12. 2019: Violent wind all night long. It kept me awake all night long. The cable I received from Julia kept me awake all night long. Fuck is wrong with this woman. She sounds more like a flapper soaked in sadness. But quietly compelling especially with her Glasgow accent. A very playful lip service exercise. I think she intentionally wanted to make me feel awkward because I haven't heard something so light and delightful like her Glasgow accent. Her cable was so flirty and I totally recommend it for readers who are tired of lemon-like-novels. However there is a familiar feeling at play here. I like to consider it edgy and rebel at heart. She wants me to go crazy. She also wants me to make this book a word salad that uses counter culture buzz words and cliche critiques. A very much of a product of beat culture without actually saying anything new but just repeat everything over and over again until one flew over the cuckoo's nest which happens to look like me. Bitch…She wants me to go insane. It appears life is strange and so compelling in "Blood And Guts In Jail." Wait to see what I bring next… Great poetic stuff that can be dark and tough to read a point…something shocking. This morning very cold and blowy. I can fell a rather strange and cold winter coming and that's bad news for my jail life. There's never been a better time to be in jail. Fuckin hell. Spending time in jail during the winter and in the middle of fuck-knows-where it must be something. Wait to see how my book it will sound…In time with the weather of course or more like hell on high water. But there's other things that kept me awake during the night. I need to take a breathe of fresh air before I spit it all out. I admit I have a problem with accepting being in jail especially the shit that happens right now in my life. Problems with Julia. Problems with the jail food. Problems

with this cell. Problems. Problems. Problems. Mostly because prison is such a weird and straightforward transitory place for me and I simply can't allow myself to live in this misery. Did I told you this place stinks? I have such a hate for this place. And fuck this bed. It's all ugly, smells bad, hard on my bones and full of bed bugs. When I have to go to bed is like I'm going in hell. I sometimes just stay on the chair and I do it for one or two days. I stand up. I walk for a bit, mostly wall to wall and is annoying because is such a short distance…only two meters both ways, I then sit down again. I write. I stand up. I walk. I sit. Such a fucked up life. Seriously depressing. I'm telling you don't get the jail. AVOID. Or at least don't come in this cell. Tell them you have a preference. Tell them you want a custom built cell with all the shit that makes you happy. You know…large TV, cable satellite, small kitchen, perhaps a fridge with a few cold beers, bunch of snacks and unlimited Netflix. Tell them. Oh lord…do a miracle, make it a holly one so i can write my book and get the fuck out of here. ALIVE. And I also want to sell a million copies and sell them like fresh apples from the garden of eden. Actually, make it one hundred million copies. You heard me Lord? Baptise my words with your holly spirit. I could do so much with all that pile of cash. I could finally afford to own all my favourite NFT's. Cats, Apes, Punks and all the stars in the Metaverse. Is what makes me happy these days. Seriously, I need a glass of water for it's not me talking, it's my meds. It appears one flew over the cuckoo's nest again. And it looks just like me. Strange looking whether outside. Violent wind. Rain will come very soon. Looking forward for that holly water. Need to baptise all my sins. Shit, rain came into my cell. The wind blew it all over the place. Lord…Is it you? Are you trying to communicate with me? "Yer aff yer heid ya doaty dobber, Shut ye geggie! I'll ride ya in tae battle with ma wee Bible, Ya ain't get yer holly water until ya send an apology to yar wee girl. The gospel of the lord speaking."

9. 12. 2019: Strange looking weather today. The wind just got violent. Tiny particles of snowflakes here and there. Winter is coming. God help me stay alive. Rather sad in my cell today, I'm hoping I will not lose my mind. So depressing here. I feel so lonely. This cell just makes everything so much worse. Days gets smaller, nights are long and boring. Night time comes in a fraction of a second here up north in Shetland and because is so cloudy outside, middle of the day is more like in the middle of the night and that's bad news for my writing. These motherfuckers shut down my light. There's barely any light in my cell. My only spark for natural light is somewhere in the early hours of morning, maybe a couple of hours but not more. I realised night comes rather fast because of the island location. I'm in the upper north of north sea. Probably very closer to Iceland. I know this because at school I always loved geography classes. Knowledge put at good use in jail. My writing just flows during the night time. I like writing in the night time. Back at home I was doing all my music work also in the night time. Everything I do creative I do it well in the night-time. During the day-time I like to sleep and I do it intentionally so I can forget I'm in jail but I also observed jail time flies quite fast during the day. Back at home I was sleeping half a day then the rest of it I was spending it in the park and sometimes at the cinema. I like to go watch movies. God damn it I shouldn't mention that for I now think how much I miss my telly. No creative juices today. Very quiet

here with nothing but just the sound of wind blowing between the empty walls of my cell. This atmosphere can have a particularly strong deterrent effect on my mental health. It's more like a discouragement from thinking positive. Perhaps write something pleasant? Some positive stuff?...I don't know the word positive anymore. Since in jail I forgot how is to be positive. I am unable to think positive. I am unable to function positive. I have no idea what it means to be positive anymore. The deterrent effect this cell is having on me is bizarre. It creates bizarre excessive thinking and I'm not feeling well. Fuckin white rabbit...obsessively keeps coming into my cell. And I told you I don't like colour white because is the same colour like the walls in my cell. Wait...the rabbit is now turning yellow. Now is green. Red. Yellow. Green. Yellow. Red. Green. It now becomes black. Fuckin rabbits all over the place and is already not much place in my cell. Feels more like a traffic jam with rabbits. "Help!!! Take the rabbits out from my cell." No one heard me. Fuck off all of you from my cell. Fuck off. Strange. They all disappeared instantly. I am hallucinating. It was only a small bug on the floor. Never seen white bugs before. I stand up. I walk for a bit...mostly wall to wall. I sit down again. I stand up. I walk. I sit. Such a fucked-up life in jail. Seriously depressing. I hate this place. And fuck this bed. It's all ugly, smells bad, hard on my bones, and full of bed bugs. How on earth I can get some good quality sleep when this bed is shit. When I have to go to bed is like I'm going to have a bath in bed bugs. You ever had a bedbug bite you before? It's fuckin disgusting. You'll go full potatoes. You'll scratch the skin for hours. Small motherfuckers sucks the blood out of you. They also leave behind blisters. I think inside the blisters are their eggs. Oh my jail days...I need to take a seat and I might sit on this chair for at least two days. Too afraid to go to bed. I feel very distressed. Chaos style. Some white bugs on the floor are moving. I think are termites or moths. Fuck this place. Now it causes me even more concern. On further inspection of the floor I noticed there was quite a few of these little white fuckers, crawling all over, there was also some more under my bed and some on my blanket. This jail sucks. Warning! Bunch of rabbits keeps coming back in my cell and changes colours at all times. It causes me concern. My sanity not the rabbits. 68 more days to go. 32 just gone. I have here everything I need on the wall. Every day I cross a line over one number. Today I crossed number 32. Of course I need to keep an eye on my jail days. I can't afford to stay longer that my sentence. I go full potatoes in World War 2 style if these motherfuckers are keeping me a day more. I'll bring the chaos in this jail. "You fuckin bastards! You heard me? I hope you all fart spaghetti Bolognese." I'm sure absolutely nobody gives a shit to what I just said. Not even a foot step on the corridor. No sound. Just silence. Oh for fuck sake...I need a holiday and a large glass of wine. I note this in my diary. It is important for me to keep a record of my best wishes for my libration day. By that time I will became a useless sack of yankee dankee doodle shit. It's jail-a-clock. Time to go on a adventure with myself and with the bed bugs. I'll get some fresh air first. Very cold and blowy outside. Already an inch of snow. Back in the cell. Back to the window. Back in the cell. Back to the window. I'm doing these movements at least a thousand times per minute. Small square ugly cell I can barely move around. The reality is that I'm at the point of inevitable consequences of deluded thinking. In my famous story I exist trapped in a cell, facing a dirty white wall. Dirty from excessive thinking. In front of me is a shadow that looks just like my moving figure. I gave this shadow a name so I can make up stories for it. Over time this shadow becomes my only sense of reality with both, the inside & outside world. I'm afraid when I will be released from jail this false view of the world I created will follow me and perceive it as true reality for the rest of my life, never having the chance to escape the shadow I created in jail. The real truth is I am manipulated by the evil who just happens to look like me. Oh well…at least now I know who to fight with for the next 68 days. An exceptional role behind bars. I might even be nominated for some exceptional work of fiction which will prove my book prize and it's this shadow on the wall who will take the credit for.

10. 12. 2019: Violent wind all night. Today rain and it comes with small particles of ice. I have no idea what on earth weather is this. Strange weather. Last night I slept with the blanket over my head and I could hear blows of wind blasting the walls of my cell. When I woke up found an inch of snow on my window. Some got into my cell. I keep the window open at all time to not die from this ugly smell of…whatever it is. Ammonia or chlorine. It comes from the toilet and the toilet is one meter from my bed. If I close the window it will only take a fraction of a second to get intoxicated. Sometimes it feels more like a gas chamber from Natzi's Germany 1943. Oh lord have mercy of me…help me get out alive. Today is very cold and blowy in my cell. I could do with an extra blanket. The only blanket I have I wear it at all time. It's full of bed bugs. It's okay. They keep me warm. Motherfuckers…they suck the life out of me. Fuck this jail.

When I get out I will go straight to a tanning saloon to cover all my my bites. All over my body I have scars. Thousands of small little red dots from bedbugs bites. They are very Itchy and arranged in a rough line all over my body. Itchy bite marks on the face, neck and arms. Itchy bite marks on my dick. Tiny bite marks on my balls. And most recently tiny bite marks on my ass. Fuck this place. I look like I've been used for some popular sports game, but used as a target and the whole gamut of creatures having a go on me. I'm telling you…this jail sucks. By the way…earlier today received new cable from Julia. It seems to me this woman is reading my thoughts. She's also feeling a little agitated. Perhaps because these days she's as lonely as my jail days and she misses me. It's okay. I am too as lonely as some of her apples & oranges found on the kitchen table. I miss my morning fruit salad. Yes I do. Let me open the letter and read it to you. It says it was sent thru the e-mail a prisoner correspondence. Local jail cable. I don't care. As long as I get something to read daily it's fine. It starts with…yes, it's a good start. The usual bipolar wee little puss. "Ya are a man-hating, man-blaming sleeveen of a devil-worshipping maggot and a moron who won't shut up. Ya fuckin pocket monkey. Fuck off." The end of the later. Girl, but what have I done to you to hate me that bad. I'm just in jail doing my time. I don't even know what she's up to. You know what? Tonight, when the clock strikes midnight, all the evil things in the world will have a full sway on her unless she's working out her tone. But she won't do it. She needs feelings, dreams and material to make her think. Can be dark and tough without. I'll just leave her be and get on with my jail days. But I kinda need her as my heroine for an experimental fiction class.

11. 12. 2019 ..e-mail a prisoner. Copy...Julia to cell 13

Ya fuckin weirdo. Ya want me for yar experimental fiction class? Ah'll ragdoll ye if Ah get ye! Bilt ya rocket or I bile yer heid with tha Lorne sausage. Eh? Ya want ma muney? Yeah, yeah, yeah, ya singing pocket monkey! Shut ye geggie! Yer aff yer heid? Ya doaty dobber! Ain't give ya any muney. Fuck off!

12. 12. 2019 ..e-mail a prisoner. Copy...saint Isaac, cell 13

Dear Julia,

I'm thinking about you right now and I've been thinking about you for days...why on earth you bring me these gloomy news? It's already gloomy weather in my cell and I have to live with it for the next 67 days. Why you doing this to me? Your cables it's causing me a bad mood...I feel low in spirits. I now have my face gloomy and my lips compressed but I guess my unhappy look won't struck you. I'm not going to stop writing to you cause then I'll be away from this directness, this unhappiness, this isness which is. I need you as my heroine for an experimental fiction class. At the same time I'm never going to have anything to do with you again. Because you, even if it is just cause of circumstances, won't love me. However, I'm willing to give you one last chance and you better not trick me with a lip-service kiss. I'm sick of being nice to you and you being a she-devil to me. Let me rub my crotch...god damn bedbugs, I have bites all over me. Listen girl... it seems to me you will never love me nor you want to give me what I want...your heart. What's the matter with you dummy, are you on your period or something? Bipolar wee little puss...talk to me nicely. With those cables you gonna be a creep. And that Glasgow accent...I ain't understand a thing. Girl...I love you. Flesh it all out. Here for you with open arms. I miss you.

13.12.2019 ..e-mail a prisoner. Copy...Julia to cell 13

Why aren't ya grabbing my cunt every chance you get? Ya slob... Don't ya see anything? I'm sending ya signals every time I write ya so that you want to own me but without own anything. Ha! Ha! Ha! You shod take me out to dinner. You knaw. Just saying. And I wrote "knaw" just because I'm saying. I'll rub ya crotch. Ya got bedbugs bites? I'll give ya special cream. You better get out of jail faster...I just want to stick my cunt into something. These days I'm as lonely as your jail days and it affects my cunt problem. ...And why are you telling me you want to be friends with me? Ya want me? Yeah, yeah, yeah. Ya wee bawbag! Then ya need grabbing my cunt every chance you get. Understand? It's a thing. Otherwise I'll fuckin dump ya for a wee bottle of buckfast. I miss ya.

14. 12. 2019 ..e-mail a prisoner. Copy...saint Isaac, cell 13

Dear Julia,

Just why are you fuckin with me? I'm sick of being nice to you.
That's why I'm giving you 24 hours to start questioning your mood.
Come out you rotten evil bitch and let's define sexuality in "Blood
And Guts In Jail." I love you so very very much. P.S, Are you fuckin
someone else right now?

15. 12. 2019 ..e-mail a prisoner. Copy...Julia to cell 13

Ya wee bawbag! Ha Ha Ha! Yer aff yer heid? I won't fuck with you
anymore cause you like the smell of my cunt. This is the only way I
can directly speak to you cause you're autistic and I'm brunette, I'm
skinny, I'm rich, and I'm a little bit of a bitch. Plus, you"ll never have a
penny to support me. Stick to ya new girlfriend...righthand! Ya still
jerk off thinking of me? Ya fuckin weirdo! Last night I imagine your
cock-bone inside my cunt-bone. And I'm only saying just to drive
you crazy. You knaw. It's like that song from the radio...A a aaa a a
a...Ooo o...And I wrote "knaw" cus i wanted to. Ya wee pocket
monkey! Ha, Ha, Ha. Ya hard now? Tell me how ya feel when ya
jerk off thinking of me! I'm thinking of ya right now! I'm crazy for
ya! Winter time in Glasgow can be hard without ya! Looking forward
to see ya! I miss ma wee boy! Ya miss me?

P.S, Ya just another wee man and you don't mean shit to me. Ha,
Ha, Ha. Ya wee bawbag!... yer new girlfriend...righthand. Ha, Ha,

Ha. Ya fuckin weirdo! Here, highly polished wood coffin for ya book. Say something!

16. 12. 2019 ..e-mail a prisoner. Copy...saint Isaac, cell 13

Dear Julia,

Your cable really upset me. You are a she-evil bitch and I'm being a baby as usual. Probably because I love you. And my love for you has no complications, no shades, no hues...Wait, let me rub my crotch. The fuckin bedbugs...I have bites all over me. Yes, as I was saying... my love for you is unconditional. I love you so very much to want to hate you. This is my poem to you. Do me a favour and stop cable me for at least few days. Just leave me the fuck alone. I've got shit to do...write a very funny book for my readers who also happens to have shit to do, swear words galore and likes to laugh at crap TV series. From now on cable me softly. And please be nice with me. This is the only way I can directly speak to you cause I'm autistic and you're a she-evil bitch. Fuck off!

17. 12. 2019: This jail sucks. When I get out I will embark on a road-trip. I need to get the jail out of me. Need a proper detox. Oh God... help me get out alive. 40 days done. 60 more to go. Winter is already here and I stay with a broken window. Today I tried to stick my head out the jail window and I knew is dangerous as well as being stupid because I had to force the window to get it wide open. The problem was the frame. It cracked. The whole thing, window &

frame felt on me from the inside. I wasn't hurt for the whole thing is rather small, about about half a meter wide. I just hid it under my bed. If any of the guards ask me where is the window I'll just tell them it disappeared in the middle of the night. Actually let me mark this in my diary. It is important for me to remember what to say...if not I'll just say something that comes first to my mind. The problem is winter is here and it sucks to have a broken window in jail. Better stay in cold than getting gassed from that fuckin toilet. I mean... cmon...it's ridiculous to sleep with a pile of shit near your bed. I have a headache from that smell. By the way it start snowing again. Already two inches on my window. Better prepare to make a snowman in my cell. Will update soon. Just flipping thru my diary and it's good news. Already fat as a baker's dog. So far I think I've done an impressive work of deconstruction of the self by means of literary madness. I covered literary anything...or at least something. I revisited classics and avant-garde works, give shape to the author's memories and revealed never seen behaviour of his famous heroine. I even covered strippers, prostitutes, artists, lovers, moments of complete madness, both, in jail and from the outside, ecstatic stuff... and I done it at least every five pages. I done it with a derelict dialect. I tore apart inner conflicts and desires that fuelled the author's creativity as a writer and I also played cards with his heroine by continuously switching identity and genre, until the author becomes a punch in the gut in the mystery and romance category. I admit I wanted to write this book in a violent, poetic, cathartic writing but to do that I also needed the right heroine. Tormented (her past), talented, educated, sexually ambivalent, brilliant, quite a bit mentally unstable, full of contradictions...You know, the sort of person I should probably avoid like the plague, because she tend to awake some dormant aspects of my personality that really should stay where it belongs. And it invariably ends badly. She was everything "Blood And Guts In Jail" needs. So far I think I've done my bit. I'm just a clown who's feeling down, except that I don't have clown shit or cosmetics to look like one. Going to sleep. Nothing else to do. Tomorrow I might have a soft spot for another story. As does experimentation. If not I'll write about me. I know, I know. I'm just a clown who's feeling down, except that I don't have clown shit to look like one.

18. 12. 2019: Just woke up and found small pack of food labeled "not for human consumption." I don't even know what that means. Found it on the floor. These days they tend to leave my food on the floor. They throw a couple of slops in a plastic bowl, add some bread, they don't bother about a fresh glass of water because the tap water smells like shit and they know I could do with a glass of fresh water at least once a week, and slip all that on a tray in my cell. Most bread is hard as a rock. The porridge sometimes is alright although is made with cold water and it kinda affects my mental health. Checking this can. It appears to be my lunch for today. The label it says: howl, howl. And there's a small puppy face. Motherfuckers… they're having a laugh at me. I've just been given dog food. I open the can, take a good look inside and it appears to be some brown sauce and chunks of meat. I taste the whole thing and…it's actually alright. It taste like…I don't know. More like cold dog food. Fuck it…I'm just gonna have the whole thing. Nobody is

going to know I ate dog food in jail. There's also some old bread that came with the dog food but the bread rather mouldy. Probably from being expired for so long. When I broke it in half found small webs of spiders in it. Some spider eggs too. It's alright...It will go well with the dog food. After further inspection around the food tray I found a small pack of dried soup. Powder based and this stuff supposed to be mixed with hot hotter. Is what it says on the label. Definitely for human consumption. I'll have it with cold water and when I drink it I will just think about my best days. Eventually everything passed down the throat quite well and now I'm ready to write because I feel alright. It's probably from the dog food. Howl, howl. Just saying. Actually...just barking. And I barked just because I'm saying. Must be from the dog food. I must tell you something about my food. The worst part was seeing an ugly spider egg inside the bread. I closed my eyes and pass it down the throat. It tasted far worse than the dog food. So far dog food is my favourite jail food. You wanna know something else? When I was a child I ate dog poo. Serious stool shit. And I was caught in the act two times. First time I was observed eating dog poo by a dog itself. The dog talked to me and said that he is a serious stool eater and he's doing it out of habit and I shod probably do it too. He also told me is drinking from the toilet, rolling in swamp muck, licking his butt, and he's doing it out of habit and I shod probably do it too because is a normal way of obtaining key nutrients, especially poop eating and butt licking. After I done it for a couple of times got parasites for a month and kept on drugs and steroids. And you know what? The dog food I had today kinda takes me back to these old days. A million people who happens to read this will feel capricious to my story...just as a capricious person does....rolling in swamp muck. I don't remember when I was caught in the act for the second time. It's probably in jail earlier today. Time to roll in the swamp with the bed bugs. Howl, howl.

19.12.2019: Today violent wind. Sometimes rain, sometimes snow, sometimes strong wind. Sometimes, sometimes, sometimes. Sometimes I'm thinking if I will ever have the ability to produce the next Dostoevsky's work. "Wha? Ya drunk or something?" I'm sorry but that's my internal chatter. I'm perfectly alright. Currently on jail water and few vitamins who happens to be my prescribed medicine for today. Today I had the chance to flip thru Dostoevsky's Demons. I asked the prison guard for a book and I was given this one. At first it appeared to be a very hard read. I'm 199 pages in and so far texts are lurid and full of mystery, psychological stuff and metaphysical twists and turns. Not an easy book to digest. In the past I think I flipped thru a few of his other works. But in "Demons" I got the chance to examine moral nihilism. Now bare with me for I'm an amateur on this topic. If I put this into context and the context is all about me then a moral nihilist would say that taking drugs for whatever reason is neither inherently right nor inherently wrong. The meta-ethical view of this is that nothing is moral or immoral but whatever is constructed by the human mind and for the very simple reason that is there to know. In "Demons" moral nihilism It becomes a very hot subject and is put down by a conspirator named Pyotr Verkhovensky. I think is Dostoevsky's male version of his heroine. The whole novel is damn good. Plot after plot after subplot and subplots from already multiple created subplots. Very hard to read book. Definitely a very hard to write book. Highly sophisticated. Dostoevsky is a mastermind at providing insight to characters and their backgrounds and personalities. I'm overwhelmed by the way he does storytelling. When I read his stuff I feel more like a singing pocket monkey. Although I'm more about documenting my life in jail on a "exactly-what-is-happening-basis" rather than write the everyday novel you find on the bookshelf. Jail food just arrived. It's fuckin shit. I'm just gonna have the bread only. Won't even bother to look what's inside the bowl. Some green liquid. Must be jail soup but it looks more like alien blood. One day I will enjoy really good food. That day it will be in 57 days from now if my counting is right. Just flipping thru some of the material I wrote for the past month. A huge pile of notes. Piles of paper in front of me on my jail table. I'm telling you if I was about to put all that into the book then it will be a brick and a half...considering that the brick weighs at least five kilos and the other half weighs just as the same which means the other half must be made from ready mix concrete rather than compressed clay. Although both might weight just the same. Complex math shit done in jail. The thing is that a good amount of stories will definitely make it into the book. Whatever will be left on the side I might sell them as non-fungible tokens also known as NFT's that's because is a way of turning artists into capitalist assholes and why not take a bite from this opportunity to make the world a better place? How sweet — now artists can become little capitalist assholes as well. Forgive my cynicism...I'm feeling too positive right now because I have finally found a way to make money on the outside. I am trying to keep an open mind on how to punch someone in the gut but in the right category. Mostly various artists, influencers and celebrities...

including me. I now have this book and I will definitely be shelved in some category along the few. It's all good. We are all a little bit of capitalist assholes...including me. I cant say I'm satisfied with my life until I write my second book. Another mad scientist, another story, another book. And this one with the most fantastical split personality that's ever been committed to paper and it also happens to look like me. The one pictured bellow truly is nicknamed as..."a mad scientist from Blood And Guts In Jail'...sold NFT.

20. 12. 2019: Here comes another day and in jail absolutely everything is the same. The tea is different today. It tastes like...don't know, it's just very salty. Motherfuckers. First, they gave me dog food. Now they messed-up my tea. They added salt instead of sugar. I told them precisely I want one spoon of sugar. They done the opposite. Added one spoon of salt. Now it tastes like seawater. Drinking seawater can be deadly to my writing. I will urinate all over my diary with less intelligent words, grammar mistakes, and a rare form of split personality that can also harbour a parasite in the Oxford dictionary. Today I'm wearing my new jail clothing. A proper style. Part of the reason I wear this style is because nobody cares once in jail. From today my everyday outfit is orange. Before I was wearing striped pyjamas that goes by the colour grey as of ashes or lead. If you ever come across jail then don't be so quick to want to lose the orange because you'd just blend in with the grey. The idea of wearing orange & grey is to bring about internal discipline. Quite different compared to what I was wearing on the outside. Mostly blade runner on a hipster style. A trend defined by a rare form of originality. Red socks, denim shirts, blue jeans, graphic tees, v-necks, hoodies, cardigans, and most recently stuff that gets the attention to go viral online. You know...like one of my often congratulated story from "Blood And Guts In Jail ." But I guess this will be more appealing to poets and writers than book readers looking for discounts on cheep wine.

21. 12. 2019: I keep write random words that leads to sentences, then sentences into paragraphs, and paragraphs into daily entrances. Eventually it turns out to be a bunch of astonishing stories. There's no order nor sanity but just chaos and insanity. Does it scares me to keep push it with my writing? I go forward and capitalise the shit out of this jail. My sentence is too short to be afraid to have a voice. Plus, I have here with me a brilliant shadow on my wall that happens to look like me. For the past few weeks It helped me put pen and paper on good use. I mean...it helped me put a brilliant brain on good use. But like any other brain, mine has become solid in a vacuum pack but still intact and it also wants to become the next Fitzgerald. "Wha? Ya drunk or sumething? Fitzgerald?" Ya wee bawbag! Ha Ha Ha!" I'm sorry but that's my internal chatter. I'm perfectly alright. Currently on jail water and few vitamins who happens to be my prescribed medicine for today. Checking the numbers...it says 55 days to go until I get out. My numbers are always right. Every day I mark an entrance in my diary and I also scratch the wall to keep a record of my days in jail. I learn that from "Cast Away," a movie I like. It tells the story of a man with no way to escape from a desolate island after a deadly plane crash. If I flip the story it kinda resonates with me so much for I too crashed on a island. Oh lord have mersey of all of me and not just my story who happens to be more famous than me. I can't imagine those serving a life sentence. It must be awful being a life time behind bars. Of course is terrifying. Imagine a draconian long-distance custody, never liberating, always a painful memory, never knowing what the next day will bring, but only living with the bad stuff in your mind, it kinda fucks up your emotional mental health. Indefinitely fucked-up for life. I'm out in 55

days and all this terror which happens to be real will stay behind me and I will pretend it never happened in my life. But because everybody else will think I'm fine I'm afraid sometimes for a while it will catch up with me again. What should I do next? Maybe get a normal job at the local bakery, sign up with love honey and get an inflatable fuck doll and live a peaceful life. I know, I know. I'm just a clown who's feeling down, except that I don't have clown shit to look like one.

22. 12. 2019: Another day. Another fight. Another chapter from my jail life and this time it broke down in the middle of the night. Not a big deal but just a fight with the bedbugs. Motherfuckers, they bit me all over my body. I haven't sign up for this shit. Bug bites are terribly irritating and it causes me a creepy experience in my writing. As you can see my writing is all over the place. These tiny creatures left me with red patches on my skin. It stings. Seriously. I feel like I've been bitten by a bunch of ants, wasps, hornets, and bees, all at once. I think I have an allergic reaction and I might require medical care. Will see how it goes this week. There's a bug on my diary. Fuck off from here. Actually I'm gonna eat it cus I'm hungry. Absolutely freezing temperature in jail. It's chilly out here today. I could do with a winter coat. Violent wind all day long. Very cold and blowy. Oh god...why I always seem to worry so quickly? I'm such a melancholic fool. I know, I know...I'm just a clown who's feeling down, except that I don't have clown shit to look like one. However, I predict my life in jail to look like one. Let me mark this one in my diary. It is important for me to know how to look for clown shit when I'm feeling down.

Terrified, mortified, petrified...stupefied by what I just said. It's the fuckin bedbugs taking life lightly over my "Blood And Guts In Jail." By the way...if it happens to get bedbugs after reading this book, don't reach my twitter asking for psychological support. Instead reach for the stars and ask for the basics of healing by reading the horoscope. Today I haven't eat anything. Jail food makes me anxious. I'm terrified when I think of jail food. Earlier I took a good look on my body and it looks very gaunt. There's a hole in my stomach. My legs are so skinny, they look like Chinese sticks. My rib cage is so visible. It's perfectly normal to be able to see your ribcage but not like mine. It's more like from a horror movie. Maybe I should try get a bit more flesh on my bones. Yeah right...from what... from thin porridge made with cold water? I'm sick of having that shit daily. Almost in all parts of my body I can feel my bones just right under my skin but I can feel them exaggeratedly, like there's almost no skin not to mention flesh. There's not much left. I'm becoming too skinny. For my lunch today I've been given one boiled egg on a silver plate but made from plastic. The plate not the egg. It will be fuckin stupid to be given a plastic egg. On the side there was a silver-spoon but made from plastic. Motherfuckers...this is usually meant as an insult..."born with a silver spoon in one's mouth." I don't feel wealthy and privileged in jail. What worries me the most is the smell of the egg. It's off. Fuck it. Straight in the toilet with it. I'll just have the bread and the bread is fucked-up too. It's okay. I'll have the plastic plate. Hey you know what? Maybe I shod just hit the plate in my head until I come up with something better to write. So far my writing sucks. Going bankrupt like the old blockbuster. I know, I know. I'm just a clown who's feeling down, except that I now have a silver spoon in my mouth. It makes me look like a wealthy and privileged clown. Aren't you curious how to look like one? Try dog food. But try it with Chinese sticks. Close your eyes and repeat: I'm amazing. I'm beautiful. I'm unique.

22. 12 .2019: Clown shit.

23. 12. 2019: Woke up in the middle of the night. The loneliness I experience in this cell it sucks every drop of life out of me. Can't sleep. There's a bunch of worries going thru my head and it doesn't let me sleep. One of the worries is the jail food. That shit makes me terribly ill...it already made an unforgettable impact on me. Everything else is just one big worry. Jail life in generally is one big worry. Terribly cold today. Wind blows in my cell. Sometimes i stare at walls and imagine how the wind smashes in each corner. The thing is it can become quite hallucinating. I tend to imagine something the shape of a ball that hits the corners of each wall and I sometimes imagine this to be quite fast and my cell is already small. Most times I have a hard time to keep up with that imaginary ball. Such is the power of mind boggling games behind bars. I would rather prefer a Nintendo playing Tetris. Oh...and that shit also makes seriously spooky noises. The wind not the Tetris. Talking about the wind. It's more of a dog whistle style. When it's dark...I'm delighted. The next thing I wish is to die. That frightened I am. This cell must be the worst environment in the history of literature to write a book. It got me a sleep disorder or some rare health condition I'm currently not aware of. I think the time is somewhere closer to 3:00 a.m. I can tell by the way the moon is positioned. It is lower in the sky. I once read a book on planetary science and it says that in the winter the moon is lower in the night sky, especially after midnight and away from the sun during the day. I'm guessing is somewhere around 3:00 a.m. Thinking to get out of bed and do some writing. Anything really. Just write something in my diary. But when I think how cold is in my cell it gives me a headache. My mouth is dry and my temples troubles me from too much thinking. I need a glass of water. Or

maybe just go back to bed and imagine listening to that Detroit house track, "Lift him up." And forget about the water for it stinks anyway. When I wake up I'm going to rise higher than I ever been before just because of that track. If not I'll try something else... probably listen to a famous Russian artist on the radio. In Soviet Union this means "Good morning my darling." She probably looks at me now like a piece of well-done steak, otherwise known as eye sex. By the way...this has nothing to do with my heroine...Julia. This is one fashionable glass of jail water staring at me from the far end corner of my table. It looks classy. I know, I know. I'm just a clown who's feeling down, except that I don't have clown shit to look like one. I have jail water.

24. 12. 2019: Man, fuck this jail. This is bullshit low life living. And fuck this bed. It's all rusty and fucked-up. Hurts my back. Motherfuckers, tiny creatures left me with red patches on my skin. The fuckin bedbugs. It stings. Seriously...I feel like I've been bitten by a bunch of snakes. As you can see I have a really hard time in jail. I'm not at all feeling happy In this place. No I'm not. It's an arctic blast at all times. I'm living in hell. Today I thought I could be a little happier. Apparently is Christmas day or Christmas Eve. Just received a mini Christmas cake from one of the guards. No idea why but apparently It supposed to make me feel happy. No. I'm not feeling very happy at all. Deep inside me all I want is to abruptly have a sensation of slapping my face, pull my skin off, twist my head, bite my hands, remove all my teeth, cut my dick and watch myself bleed until "death-me-a-part." If this would be the easiest way out of jail...

in a coffin or alive then i'll take it. I just can't take it anymore in this way. Shivering cold today. The temperature in my cell must be way below zero. It's very chilly out here today and I could do with an extra blanket. Violent wind all day long. Very cold and blowy. Weather forecast from behind bars doesn't look too well. Nothing else to do but just stare in the corner of a blank wall. I'm just looking out the window and the sky looks weird. The sky above the jail looks like the colour of a television turned to a dead channel. Serious spook shit. Going back to bed. Nothing else to do. Feeling very uninspired. This must be the worse Christmas I had in my entire life. I'm crying the soar grapes.

25.12.2019: Merry Christmas. I wish you all happiness and joy, but above all this I wish you to never get the jail. If you do get the jail then don't try look like me... a bunny-hugger on a school strike. It's what it says on my prisoner ID.

26. 12. 2019: Just another fucked-up day in jail. And you know what's even more fucked-up? Yesterday it was exactly like today and tomorrow it will be exactly like yesterday. Yesterday it was Christmas day and tomorrow it will be just another fucked-up day in jail which means today is as fucked-up as tomorrow, and tomorrow it will be exactly like today. Man, fuck this jail. This is bullshit low life living. I never felt so incredibly depressed. This jail sucks. I have a constant feeling of my energy being sapped. My enthusiasm being dampened. My passion being depleted by the effect this jail has on me. I have become an unhappy and emotionally damaged man. There must be a way to keep a happy knack at least once every five days. If I can do that then I might get out a perfectly sane man. I need to stay focused. Just looking out the window and the sky it looks pretty much like yesterday. More like the colour of a television turned to a dead channel. I told you today it will be exactly like yesterday and tomorrow it will be just like today. Unfortunately It's how it is. Bitter arctic weather in my cell. I haven't seen any more bedbugs. I think they're all dead because of the cold. Good. Oh god...there's a bad taste in my mouth. The most common reasons must be from those off eggs. Jail food at its worse. When I open my mouth It smells more like a cadaver. So embarrassing. I haven't washed my teeth since two months. And I also stink. When I smell my jail clothes it's like sticking my nose in a pig's ass. For some reasons I emit a strong and offensive odour stank of ammonia, chlorine and dirt. All three at the same time. It's the fuckin jail smell and is in every cake layer of my cell. Nothing but just an ugly smell. Seriously unpleasant. I could do with a wash. But where? In the sink? I'll die in five seconds in this arctic blast. The water is freezing cold. I don't even have

something to keep warm. No thanks. I'll stick with the stinky jail clothes. In fifty days I will get a proper wash. Classic jail behaviour.

27.12.2019: Today is just another fucked-up day in jail. Guess what? Yesterday was as much as fucked-up like the day before and today it will be exactly like yesterday, which means tomorrow it will be exactly like today, and today it will be as much as fucked up like the day after tomorrow. Man, fuck this jail. This is bullshit low life living. I need a fuckin glass of wine, full English breakfast, toast, cup of green tea, marmalade, some sex, tattle and soul. And I want to have it all with a silver spoon until I shock and seduce the literary world. Whatever that might be. I just want to give my work the power to mirror the reader's soul. Wait a second...the pipe got frozen in my cell. That is serious clown shit. Huge chunk of ice is covering the sink. I had to lick the ice for a few drops of water. Can you believe that? My last days in jail it seem to be more of a torture. What's next? An alien room-mate? Today I've been looking again for bedbugs. I haven't seen any of them. I think they're all dead because of the cold. Good. Oh god...there's a blast of wind hitting each corner of my cell. I sometimes tend to look for it but never manage to catch it. Fast motherfucker. Scanty looking cell with a few frayed notes from my diary tacked to the wall, a stainless steel toilet, a frozen sink, and an ugly bed full of bedbugs. That's my home. At least the bedbugs are dead. But they might come back to life if it gets warm. Today I have experienced a serious problem. It's about my teeth. My teeth started to decay very badly. I know exactly what caused this. The fuckin jail food. There's pain around my gums. It feels sore, swollen and at times my gums it bleeds. Been spitting blood for the past few days but today got serious. Not my mouth. Not my beautiful teeth. Oh god...I'm going crazy. I did lost one tooth. It fell out while I was eating. I barely felt anything. I almost swallowed some of the tooth with bread. For some reason it cracked very easily. When I took a good look at it was full of plaque around the edges. Definitely the jail food done this to me. If not the dog food. Howl howl. When i get out it will be worth getting a set of brand new teeth and wear them like a fashion statement. One of those sparkling white teeth which will cost me an arm and a leg. A pair of fake teeth glued under my missing teeth. Another option it will be to drink a can of petrol, then, lit up a cigarette and wait for the fireworks to lighten up the sky. It will be the greatest closing for a novel. I told you the secret is in the stars. It's all good. The universe smiles upon me. Cheese!

28. 12. 2019: Today, tomorrow and for many days to come I will still be around the afterglow of these uninspiring days in jail which is among the finest of the English literature because of my views on the subject of life in jail. In friendly terms speaking this is what happens when you get bitten by thousands of bed bugs. It force you to make good use of imagination...eventually gives life to useful words on paper. To be honest, in jail I thought of myself more like a telegraph operator than a prisoner. Finally, it led to the discovery of becoming a writer. I have absolutely no idea how all this happened. Perhaps it just meant to be this way. Get the jail, write a book, make a million bucks, buy a bunch of NFT's and become friends with Elon

Musk. I just wanna ride with him to the Mars via rocket producer SpaceX. But first need to make sure I get out of jail alive. Mars can wait. Thank god the bedbugs are lost. They all got frozen. Good. Taking a good look out the window and I can see a sparkling clean night sky. It's nearly night time but still a bit of sunset left. A small piece of sun is still visible at the far end of the horizon. These days it's getting dark very soon up here in north. In the winter time it appears the light never shines properly on Scotland, it's a dark land full of mythical beasts and strange supernatural folk. It says in the bible. I don't know if this has something to do with less light during the day. But I know the Haggis is a ferocious animal with two short legs on its left hand flank and two longer ones on the right. This makes it ideal for running around the hills of Scotland on low light. I read that in a letter given to me by one of the prisoners from wing A. It's were they keep the ones who flew over the cuckoo's nest. Signed, The Loch Ness Monster, our pet for brief appearances to increase the tourist trade in Scotland. I haven't said this. It says on the letter I was given. Got dark outside. I'm trying to portray the perfect killer sky on a freezing night. I might have to remember this on a cruise when I transit the Atlantic. Hopefully it will not sink. Oh wow...you shod see how beautiful it looks the ocean from my jail window. I've never seen a painting that captures the beauty of the ocean at a moment like this. Definitely my most memorable moment in jail. Sunset, cold cup of tea, and an open sea. I do get a good view of the sea from my window. It's the only good thing that happened to me in this jail...the view from my window. It's quite alright actually. When I return at the window I tend to forget how this jail is killing me. More like killing me softly. Looking very picturesque over the hills of

Shetland. Will spend the night looking out the window and imagine Disney-world.

29. 12. 2019: Bad news. I've just been visited by my parole officer and sadly she denied my early release for New Years Eve. This was my only chance to get out of jail earlier for I'm at the half of my sentence. According to the prison service I shod get out half way thru my sentence because...because I already served half the god that time. That's why. I told the parole officer, and by the way...she looked so young, I bet she wasn't older than my sister, and my sister is only twenty one, that I want to get smashed on coke and she thought I want to get smashed on cocaine. Definitely coke. Not cocaine. She told me..."Neah, you ain't get the coke this time. You get the jail." What? But I only wanted to drink a can of coke. That's all. She asked me..."what would you do if I approve you for early releasee?" I'm having all my coke...I said. I so miss my coke. Back home I had coke every day. Even now I still have some left in the fridge. Well, by now I'm definitely evicted from not having my rent paid. But the coke is there in the fridge waiting for me to sip a drink. When she left my cell she threw at me a shopping list. But she done it with a fling of London fashion week, like I supposed to watch her catwalk from the far end corner of my cell. On the list it was written a poem. Let me tell it to you..."I write my shopping-list in rhyme, It doesn't take me too much time, and always helps me to remember, I've been doing it since last September, wholemeal bread, low-fat spread, strawberry jam, dry-cured ham, Cheddar cheese and hard cock cum." I don't even know what that means. I'm being locked in a

crazy's people place, surrounded by the crazy, judged by the crazy. This is bullshit. Man, fuck this jail. I need a glass of water. Terribly cold today. The usual arctic blast but not even a fling of wind. Everything is very quiet. Very nice and clear sky. Almost nighttime. Nice moon. Going to bed...nothing else to do. I have to say that my days in jail are getting worse and worse day by day. I know I know... I talk again like a bunny-hugger on a school strike.

30. 12. 2019: Bad news again. This time the bad news came in the early hours of this morning. A change came over me. And this change was like a change in the weather. I become unusually ill. There's something wrong with me. I have a high temperature, a persistent cough and feeling dizzy. It feels like everything is spinning around me. I tried to get out of bed and walk towards the sink to sip some water but felt down. It feels like the cell spins with me. Seriously...I felt down...couldn't walk half a meter. Not even when I was high on drugs I felt this way. By the way...today I received a hot cup of tea and they also fixed my sink. They removed the huge block of ice. I now have running water. Very grateful. You shod see the prison officer how he was hitting the ice with a huge hammer to brake it down to pieces. In the end he also managed to damage the sink. Small piece of something that was part of the sink fell out. Well, it was working fine anyway. The water runs just fine now. For fuck sake...I'm tired of living in this misery. Can't wait to get out and return to a normal life. Fuck this jail. I ain't come back. And there's also a shortness of breath I have, more like having a difficulty with my lungs. I feel like I can't get enough air in my lungs. Very strange.

Never in my entire life felt so desperate to look for air. Spent most of the day at the window to get blows of cold air in my face. Not cus was pleasant, it's cold, but I need fresh air to get into my lungs. Feeling very strange. I can't explain how I managed to get so sick. Being sick in jail It's bad news. If you happen to die in jail, nobody gives a fuck. They'll put your body in a plastic bag and burn it at the local jail crematorium. The remains will then end up in a bin. Can you imagine that...you end up in a bin. Terrifying. Mortifying. Stupefied... End up in a bin with the dust. I better shut up otherwise I get into panic mode and my readers will too. What's even more terrifying is these thick layers of bricks found in the walls. I start to get scared when I look at them. I must be claustrophobic or something. Or perhaps is because I feel sick...I must be hallucinating. I don't know. Whatever it is I'm scared when I look at these ugly walls. I'm returning to bed. Sorry, can't write. I can't walk. I feel incredibly sick. Probably the best way to forget about this is to force myself to sleep. No bed bugs today. Good.

31. 12. 2019: I never thought I will spend New Years Eve in hospital nor in jail. Very bad news...I'm at the local jail hospital. Got the Covid-19 virus. My lungs are damaged. For the past few hours I've been feeling gradually more unwell and more breathless and here I am now handcuffed to a hospital bed. There's an oxygen mask tied to my mouth. My left hand is handcuffed to the bed frame. I can't even go to the toilet unless I have to carry the bed with me. I been peeing in a bucket and shit in the same bucket. Oh god...I want to die. I want to live. But i would also want to get out of jail alive. I'm in a

room that doesn't look like a cell but more like a hospital room. There are not much distractions here where I am. I was told it will take a few days to recover and I will have to remain in hospital for at least one week until I'm stabilised and ready to be discharged. I was far too weak to argue with the doctors that I need to do some writing so I let them be to do what they want with me. They took my diary. They took all my pencils. I was told I can't write while I am in hospital. To be treated, the doctors gave me injections which greatly alleviated my pain and the inflammation of my lungs. These injections sometimes gave me bursts of intense energy but it didn't lasted very long. However, these injections also gave me all kind of strange thoughts, it kinda troubled my mind a little. There were moments when I was hallucinating. Sometimes I couldn't make a difference of the world I am now and the world I was before. For some reason I felt much comfort in the world I was creating now. The drugs gave me reason to make sense of things I am unable to express on paper. Forget it. It's the drugs kicking in. They gave me something. Hopefully I will not transform myself into a patient that welcomes this institution as my new home. Need to stay focused. I secretly mark this entrance in my diary using an imaginary pen and paper. It is important for me to keep a record of what's happening around me. Pretending to sleep now. I stay alert. There's an alien watching me. It's staying exactly in front of me. Two blue frogs the size of a football are at my window. A turtle the size of a penny is under my bed. I'm being watched. Everything is under control. Perfectly sane and normal.

1. 1. 2020: Oh dear...take a seat ladies and gentlemen because this is gonna be weird. Breaking news. I just woke up with a dick in my hand. Motherfuckers they cut my dick while I was asleep. I didn't feel a thing. Those drugs they gave me yesterday fucked up my system. You not gonna believe but they put my dick on the side of the bed so I can take a good look at it. Probably for the last time. It's made from high quality rubber and it makes a squeaky sound and is also a little note under it. It says I could use my dick to erase pencil mistakes and there are ways I could test this out. I don't even know what that means. Probably zero procreation, then, cancer followed by death. Or...enjoy muff diving? Let me quickly send a cable to Julia.

..e-mail a prisoner. Copy...saint Isaac, cell 13

Dear Julia,

The beast is gone. I lost it. Sorry girl, I will now have to muff diving to look for oysters. It's okay. I'm professionally trained to scuba diving.

2. 1 .2020: Jesus Christ...I just had the most fucked-up dream ever. Like ever ever. I dreamed I lost my dick. Precisely...that I had my dick cut off. Can you believe that? Checking now...its all good. The beast is sleeping. As a side effect it made me shaking. I can't see myself live life without a dick. Life without a dick it sucks...what shod I say to a woman if things get spicy...probably say something like..."I have became an expert lover in other departments to cover up your lack of sleep. Fancy scuba diving?" The existential importance

of the dick is real. Oh god...It sucks in this hospital and I'm also bored out of my mind. Hospital food just arrived. It looks like shit. Mushroom with beans and a slice of bread. Cheap, low quality food. Oh wait...a miracle happened. A pack of biscuits. This food makes me think if I should get my emotional health checked. I'm having this food and back to sleep. Nothing else to do. I'm handcuffed to a bed. This place sucks. I can't wait to get out. 44 more days to go.

3.1.2020: I've got even more bad news. Woke up with a sudden blurry vision. I also think I start to see things that aren't real. I see detailed images of events, people and places. On my right side of the bed there's river Thames and a plastic duck is sailing towards a hole in the wall. Apparently the duck cannot focus on her trajectory due to an invisible object in the water also because of the imbalance of the eye muscles. Something even more crazy but it looks very real to me and I don't think I am actually crazy. Definitely not crazy...I see Jesus baptising a frog and he's doing it with both hands. It happens just opposite my bed in the river Thames. It's now with the holly spirit. The frog. Amen. When my sigh will return back to normal I will probably have to write about the events of today. And I will do it in secret when everyone is at sleep. I'm afraid someone will see what I wrote and call me a crazy. Writing crazy things in a crazy peoples place is definitely crazy and probably not a good idea for I might be labelled a crazy. The thing is I think I am a little crazy. It's probably the drugs I'm being given. Definitely the drugs. Doctors, nurses, frogs on my window, aliens behind the door, all these it's an illusion. A side effect from my treatment, making everything seem weird.

Wait...hospital food just arrived. This is my second meal for today. At least food is coming here. In jail, food was coming with the pigeon trolley...once a week. Motherfuckers, they gave me dog food then starved me for days. Let me see what I've got. It's exactly the same food like yesterday. Mushroom with beans and a slice of bread. It looks like shit. It's cheaply made, extremely low quality food. I want to take a shit on it and send it back. Oh wait...a miracle happened. Pack of biscuits. Same biscuits like yesterday. Caramel flavoured biscuits wrapped in vanilla. It says on the label. There's a picture with a baby holding a biscuit. I have no idea what that means. Must be baby biscuits. Oh dear...this food really makes me think if I should get my emotional health checked with the alien standing right now in front of me. Is looking straight at me. When I grab my food he is grabbing his dick. I have no idea what is trying to tell me. If you know anything take two aspirin and tweet me. But do it in secret. It's fucking embarrassing what's happening with me. I'm having this food and back to sleep. Like there's something else to be done. I'm handcuffed to a bed. This place sucks. Can't wait to get out. 43 more days to go and I'm out.

4. 1. 2020: I have a confession to make. Since I arrived at the jail hospital I've been lying to you at all times. I'm going to tell you the real events that occurred in my life for the past few days. I had an affair with a nurse. If you're reading this I suggest you pause everything, take a steady and comfortable seat and look for the perfect drink...preferably tea and biscuits on a traditional tray. Let me switch for BBC Two. It's where this story happens. By the way...I just had my food and it was the exact thing like yesterday. Beans on toast and pack of biscuits. As I was saying...I had an affair with my nurse. We've been shagging for the past few days. The truth is a little different. One early morning woke up in secret to look for my diary and seen this superbly beautiful nurse coming into my room with a tray. She was bringing me the breakfast. I was in so much pain that morning but as she moved closer to me I immediately got healed. It happened instant. Her good looks especially her majestic ass biscuit healed me. She was a grand looking girl of around six foot, of a proudly imposing appearance...more like a

model. I've got excited beyond belief when I seen such a good looking girl. You wouldn't believe how my productivity spiked up after I meet her. Her presence haunted me. After a couple of days we both decided to get on the sex thing. We tried at least ten sex positions. We tried the missionary and this was difficult because I was handcuffed to a bed. Doggy style from the left side and this one worked out. Legs on shoulders. Reverse cowgirl with the Bronco baseball cap. I played in the defence corner. The wheelbarrow and I had to flip the bed. Side-by-side scissors and she recommended this one because she said it is easier for her to get straight on G-Spot. I don't even know what that means. And finally...we tried the countertop sitting although it was difficult being handcuffed to a bed. She had to swivel her hips for a happy twist. She wanted me so badly that she started to make loud noises, so loud that the alien in front of me started to rub his dick. Sometimes I would completely forget I'm in jail. My time with her felt more like a religious experience. She will return to me in the early hours of each morning and bring me new paper to continue with my book writing. She told me I was to become a famous writer and she will assist me on the process of making it happen. The assistance was with mainly correcting my grammar mistakes. Sometimes during her nightshift we would have exciting sex in my bed and we will do it just to inject some passion into our lives. She will come to my bed, talk about my grammar mistakes for a bit and then go straight for sex. Sometimes we were kissing like how teenagers will do it before going to high-school, then, we will shag so much more fulfilling and exciting than any other couple ever before. Some nights she would prepare for our hospital dates, buying herself new lingerie and getting her hair done. And when we finish shagging we then immediately plan the next shag like putting it into the calendar with a very specific date, very specific hours as well very specific location around my bed. The location was very important since I was handcuffed to a bed. But the next shag was like the best shag of all shags. The most banal thing for me was when she will secretly come around my bed while I was sleeping and she would slowly get under the sheets and rub my feet with coconut cream. She would do it slow, so slow that I could barely feel any movement. She was moving like a snake. But her magic it didn't end up with just a rub. She would whisper a few words in my ear, saying that she came to bring my medicine, and she will ask me if the medicine made me feel any better, but she would also bite my ear. That was only the beginning of another sexual appetite. She was really something. I never meet a girl in my life with such a huge sexual appetite. When we've been shagging I use to orgasm very fast, sometimes I was counting to ten to see how long I would resist. That hot she was. And when we both orgasm It was like seeing ourselves living in a luxury villa on a beautiful island. A very special girl. Even more special than my girl...Julia. After just five days my life as I knew it descended into darkness. One morning paperwork arrived on my bed saying that I shod be returned to my cell. The governor decided. Motherfucker. I hope he will shit spaghetti bolognese on its way to work. When hospital staff were talking about my transfer I would carefully listen their conversation but doing so by pretending I'm at sleep and I would take secret notes of their conversation. I really wanted to see my girl one more time before I go. By now I was obsessed with her. We both had enough fairy tales to fall in love. I just wanted one more romantic fling with her even if it came in fifty shades of grey. By evening I was prepared for the worst, told to pack my stuff and off with me in the hole. Never seen my girl. But it was a five day holiday away from this hell. I will now think for a day or two how to scrap some stories from the events of my life that I've just been thru. Eventually something it will end up in my book.

5. 1. 2020: No way! This is bullshit. Bedbugs are back. These tiny creatures It will leave me again with red patches on my skin. And it stings. Seriously...It feels like I've been bitten by a bunch of snakes. I'm telling you...don't get the jail. Instead, get the night buss and a room at the Crispy Bacon Motel. It probably offers a better place for writing. Today again arctic blast in my cell. Looking out the window I can see proper snow. Bunch of rabbits running all over. It looks like they are playing in the snow. Baby ones especially. The only good thing in this jail is the view from my window. When I sit on top of my chair and take a good look out the window by natural law I turn into serenity myself. In layman language it means to accept the things I cannot change, courage to change the things I can, and wisdom to know the difference. I would love to keep an open mind to that prayer but in jail is hard to find such wisdom. Mainly the wisdom to know the difference. Wait, jail food just arrived. You've gotta be kidding. It's a fuckin joke. There's a plastic egg in my plate. It looks real. Actually wait, it's boiled. Oh dear...it smells worse than my two months old unwashed underwear. There's also the usual slop. They just drop it into a bowl and sent it out. It smells so rotten more like my unwashed feet. I think it's nearly two months since I haven't washed my feet. And if you ever wonder what is like to not wash yourself for two

months then don't. You might experience a bad day just by thinking how is like. Bed bugs are back and this time are all over the place. Fuck this jail.

6. 1. 2020: Woke up in the middle of the night and spent most of the time looking out the window until early morning. I don't think I ever starred so much at something. I mostly starred at the sea. There's not much else to see but just the sea which is half a mile distance from the jail walls and some hills that surrounds the east cost. I must admit I get an excellent view of the sea from my window. It's more like the view from a postcard. Too bad the jail is not included in the frame, it will make everything more fun. And a couple of crazy prisoners shouting out the window…"we want go home." That will be something. It will help with the sale of the postcards. A very calming sea. No blows. No wind this early morning. Can almost see the sunrise. For some reason I always loved a good sunrise in the winter. This comes from my childhood. Growing up in orphanage in my first years I experienced low mood, sadness and depression. I think It was around the age of six when my parents dropped me in, then, for the next five years I used to be kept in a small dormitory along with a dozen more children, I remember the dormitory had these tall windows with security bars on them, but I never knew why, I think to keep us in so we can't run away. Sometimes it felt more like a jail for children. They kept us for months and months in that dormitory, only an hour a day left us out and about and it was only for a quick meal, basic wash, then, back in the dormitory. It was a year later when we've been moved out to a

larger orphanage and from there we experienced a bit more freedom, gradually increased year after year. My most happy days were the ones I played with the snow in the court yard. It happen to be snowing most days I was playing. Then, in the evening do some drawings until early morning, all kind of silly drawings and I was staying awake all night until very early morning so I can catch a beautiful sunrise at a grateful universe. I'm now at the age of thirty, not playing with the snow but in jail watching the snow, and by the way, for some reason it feels like I'm back in that orphanage and watching the snow from the window. A very strange deja vu. I don't know why. It just happen to come over me. Almost sunrise now. Sunrise during the December and January months are the most fascinating for me. You get the beautiful colours of the sun over the snow and the snow turns into a sparkling white with a touch of blue. More like a light blue. This effect it happens to be in the early hours of the morning. More like seven or eight is when the snow it starts to mirror the morning sky. In jail it gives me a better sense of gratitude for my future. When I'm caught up in the natural beauty of the sunset combined with the colour of the snow I get rid of any unpleasant thoughts I live with and feel higher levels of satisfaction and gratitude for my future. It would be nice this feeling to last longer than a day. Oh god...can't wait to get out of this jail, publish my book, travel the world, play my favourite Spotify playlist, and have fun making music. I miss my music as much as I miss my DJ'ing. You bet I'm damn good at DJ'ing. When I'm out I will give it a go. A fresh new start. Rather calm looking morning in my cell. Dead calm. Absolute quiet. Total absence of noise. Not even a sound. I don't get that many days like these. Most of my days in jail are like a library of books talking with each-other and bringing all that shit into my head. All their god damn chapters into my head. Non stop speeches and they do it until I fall asleep. Sometimes even in my sleep it follows me. I don't even know where they're coming from...they just come all over me. That's how most of my days are in jail. And nights too. Today is silence in my cell. Serenity under my chair. Tranquility in the air. Everything is still in my cell. Nothing moves. Nothing is making a sound. My heart is calming down because devil is not around. I just wish all my remaining jail days to start with this kick ass attitude. It feels more like a liberation day. By the way, there's 39 more days to go and I'm out. And when I'm out, another story. Another book. Another chapter from Saint Isaac's life but this time his life on the outside. You must check that out too otherwise I'm not a happy knack.

7. 1. 2020: Some rain today. I thought It supposed to snow during the winter time. Not anymore. The snow it almost disappeared. It's all melted. Very strange weather in these parts of the world. Today there's something odd happening in my cell. It just doesn't feel right. It feels very humid. A lot of humidity in the air. It's a bit like lakes and oceans are evaporating in my cell. Large parts of my bed sheets are humid. Most people find comfortable sleeping in dry bed sheets. Fuckin jail...every day must bring some mini-punishment on me. My cell it feels naturally like hell. I'm pissed off and pissing drops of water are slowly entering my cell. Oh my days...I need to find a way to calm myself down otherwise I hang myself with bubble gum. I'm sure the house of God will not collapse on me. I say of-course to suggest that something is not right in my cell. It feels like the most common

jail problems are all over me. Again. It appears to be a condensation problem in my cell. There's all over the place water droplets and are mostly on the window and on the walls. The damp it's causing me a problem. It smells bad. And I can't do anything. I'll just keep the window wide open all day with the hope to give my little jail house a fresh breath of air before I go to sleep. Excellent idea…keep window open in the winter so I can die from a cold. I'm sorry…I'm in a state of complete unhappiness. All this caused me a terrible mood. It's cold. It's wet. It's damp. This does not make me feel good. I note this in my diary. Let me write it down: Today I feel like shit. Signed, Donkey. Wild ancestor of the wild ass.

8.1.2020: Man, fuck this bed. It's all rusty, bended all over and it hurts my back. Just woke up with hundreds of bug bites all over my body. The bedbugs are back and this time they brought the whole regiment on me. It feels like I've been bitten by the whole gamut of insects... bees, ants, fleas, flies, mosquitoes, wasps, and arachnids and it stings so badly. It really hurts. I'm crying from so much pain I'm into right now. I feel stressed and hostile. I better stay in one foot and count to ten, maybe I calm down. I'm counting. Can't believe I live this bullshit low life. It's now been two months since I'm in jail, and by the way I know for sure it's almost two months cus I marked it in my diary, the numbers don't lie, but even now I can't believe I arrived in jail. The talented Saint Isaac...now look at me...how pathetic. In jail along with the crazies. Hey, you know what? At least I got to experience the whole gamut of insects on me. I mean... common, you ain't man enough if you haven't been bitten by a bunch of bedbugs. Fuck these motherfuckers. I swear on her majesty cedar soap that if I had a lighter right now I'll burn this place down to ashes and I don't care if I get out. Actually I need to get out. It must be an intelligent question...how to get out. Obviously much exhausted by my clever thinking. I just miss a bit of sleep in a quite simple desperate human way. Too truly...I forgot how is like to sleep in a normal bed. Right now I'm into one of those moments...crazy ones. All I want is a shot of tequila and two dozen camels to drag me out from this ugly dream. If that's not possible I need a cuddle with a burning candle so I can burn till there's nothing left from me. Saint Isaac is a book.

9. 1. 2020: Oh my jail days…37 more to go and counting. I need a glass of jail water maybe I feel better cus I feel like shit. Informally like shit. The food I just had earlier made me feel crap. Had the usual egg and a bowl of slop. The egg smells like death. The soup it looks like some rare form of alien blood. It's green texture and has these lumps in between. Maybe is indeed made from alien blood because I almost look like an alien. My urine turned green and my pubic hair disappeared. Actually is all there but my vision I unclear. I closed my eyes and swallow everything from the plate. It's the only way I can have my jail food from now on. Today I've been sitting on a chair all day long. The chair i sit is made from steel and is also built in the table. I can't even move it. Must stay in the same position at all time and it sucks. My clothes are dirty and my shoes needs replacing. My hair feels greasy. My teeth are ugly. My eyes are so tired that could scare the cats. My fury is so intense that the reader will crash like broken glass. I feel incredibly bored. Hungry. Tired. Crap. Taking a good look out the window…sea calmer, thought wind shifted exactly towards my window. Crazy isn't it? Just what I thought. I wish I could have some tea and biscuits before good night.

10.1.2020: Woke up with new cable from Julia. It says…"I want you to match me on e-harmony." I don't even know what that means. Bipolar wee lil puss must be up for something. Better write her back otherwise she's taking a full swing on me.

Dear Julia,

Just had a wash in the sink and I thought to catch up with you on a highly intelligent conversation. By the way...this jail sink it sucks. There are a ton of things I dislike about this sink. I can tell you it's not pleasant to wash in the sink. I managed to wash my nails only. Each day running out of nail polish and my nails looks out of control. Back home I use to polish my nails with special Russian cream from the suburbs of the Moscow Kremlin. In jail I do it with margarine. Girl, you wanna match me on e-harmony? I think that will be a great idea. We could start from fresh. You know...you give me a couch to crash for a couple of weeks, I give you my heart and hustle when the clock strikes midnight. And I'll do it until we both achieve ultimate passion. It could be fun. By the way, I wear a clerk costume made up from jail paper. Cutaway paper coat, dark paper trousers, and a round paper cap with a small sailor-like peak. All made from paper. Can you believe that? I gave away my jail clothing for a quick wash and they gave me pepper clothing. I now have to wear paper clothing until my stuff comes back from the laundry. Aren't you feel an endearing little grin to kiss me? At least for the sake of my new outfit. I look super cool. And I also got clean shaved today. It feels good to get rid of the bunch. One thing I don't feel good about is my cell. It's a piece of crap, it smells like a pigs ass, meals are like a teacher's pet on diet, but love is in the air. Yes girl love is in the air and is all over my cells walls. I've been thinking about you lately. I never figured out how much I love you until I got the jail. Are you with me so far? Good, because I want you to do me a favour. Can you?

Can you update my e-harmony bio with "a versatile writer enjoying a bag of Dorito." It will help with our first date.

Yours faithfully, a major British novelist enjoying a bag of Dorito.

11. 1. 2020: ..e-mail a prisoner. Copy...Julia to cell 13

Ya fuckin weirdo! Ha Ha Ha! Yer aff yer heid? I won't date with you anymore cus you got tha bedbugs. Plus, you"ll never have a penny to support me. Ya wee pocket monkey! Ha, Ha, Ha. You wanna match me on e-harmony? First, ya need grabbing my cunt every chance you get. Get it? Second, ya need sending me signals every time ya see me so that you want to own me but without own anything. Third, Ya want me? Yeah, yeah, yeah. Ya wee bawbag! Ya just another wee man with a small dick and you don't mean shit to me. Ha, Ha, Ha. Buy me a gold ring and I will think about ya for a week or I'll dump ya on e-harmony. This is the only way I can directly speak to you cus I'm brunette, I'm skinny, I'm rich, and I'm a little bit of a bitch. Yours, Queen Bitch.

12. 1. 2020...e-mail a prisoner. Copy...saint Isaac, cell 13

Dear Julia,

I must say...I'm terribly disappointed by your cable. I can accept anything, except the reason that you can only exist as a parasite in my thinking. The love of a parasite is worth nothing. Right now what seems to be the easiest for me to say is....but I don't think of you anymore.

13. 1. 2020: All I did today is staring out the window with a cup of cold tea in my hand. I'm a mature man standing in a prison cell with a cup of cold tea in my hand, and staring deeply out of the window, and all I think is nothing. I guess I suppose to be working, or studying, or ticking off things on my to-do list. It can seem almost the definition of wasted time. It seems to produce nothing, to serve no purpose. This fuckin place sucks. Most people will say: "I had a great day." That's just the sort of thing people would say to one another. Not me. Talking to a wall will be a bad idea. They'll keep me here indefinitely, thinking I'm some crazy dude or something. But maybe in a better future I will do it right so I better keep stare out the window for some period of purpose-free calm and also get some ideas for what to write. Plato suggested a metaphor for the mind: our ideas are like birds fluttering around in the aviary of our brains. But in order for the birds to settle, Plato understood that we needed periods of purpose-free calm. Staring out the window offers such an opportunity. Especially the window of a jail. You will see the world going on totally different. Definitely different. Like the sound of church bells in the city once the traffic has died down at night. So you better get the jail for some purpose-free calm and don't forget to bring with you special bug cream for the bed bugs. Take two aspirin and tweet me, I might be able to recommend something else. But it will cost you an arm and a leg and a pair of sparkling white teeth. One of those fake teeth glued under missing teeth. These days I suffer from bad teeth. It's the jail food killing me softly to the point of existential crisis. Oh my jail days for I feel like I want to drink a can of petrol,

then, lit up a cigarette and wait for the fireworks to lighten up the sky. It will be the greatest closing for a novel. Don't you think? I told you the secret of never getting bored is in the stars. It's all good. The universe smiles upon all of us. Say cheese! I keep ending up staying glued to a jail window, looking at nothing, thinking at nothing. Just killing time. In jail it's the only thing you can do and it might also keep you alive. I won't recommend you get the jail. You better get the night bus and check-in at the Crispy Bacon Motel. A single night in jail is going to psychologically scar you because you're going to be victimised by other prisoners while in jail. They will bitch you and moan you with their experience and they will trot out again and again until you say something loud. Usually something you wont forget. Something that feels rather like an eternity. Something that it will make you trust people a little less than you did before. I'm talking about the negative change to your mental well-being that has been progressing downwards since you've been in jail. Again, I won't recommend you get the jail. Just got myself another cold cup of tea and it taste like shit. Did not even eat the jail food today. It's terrifying only when I look at it. Still glued to this jail window and I watch this beautiful moon who also happens to not care of me. I wonder what its creator think of me. Because if there is a creation there must be a creator (consider universe as creation.) Isn't this enough to concrete the fact that a God exists? In the bible it says that he is tall, rather narrow looking face, brown looking hair, and a nose the shape of a Catholic. His face is like a face you have not seen many times unless you got bitten by a thousands bed bugs. Oh…around my cell theres plenty of these motherfuckers. It might even restore your faith in God. To be honest, the other day I actually prayed to God to do something with this bed bugs. Kill them or something. Did not got any reply from him. Please don't laugh at this big illusion created by the author itself. We both know there is a necessity of a creator because it eludes the human mind, making it to believe there is heaven after life. What a bunch of fuckin lies. I think we can reasonably agree that is not me speaking. But somedays I amaze myself what shit I come up with in this ugly cell. Right now I'm in a state of sound sleep and I have no idea what I'm talking. The whole universe is nonexistent to me but it is present for the rest of beings. Is this real? Because I don't think I'm real. Just a fictional character created by the author.

14. 1. 2020: Heavy rain at night. More rain during the day. Am I scarred? Probably, but not what you might think. This is how it works in jail. One sunny day. One shitty day. The thing I'm most afraid of is the shit when I get out. My days on the outside it will be quite something. I have nowhere to stay. I'm broke. Actually...I have a couple of bitcoin in my saving account but don't know how to get hold of it as my digital wallet is stored on my iPhone. The phone itself is...God knows where. Shod be with my property at the jail reception. If it's missing then my journey on the outside It will be really interesting. So interesting that I'm afraid to think what will happen in my future quiz. And if my quiz is shit I can already predict my future. I could probably see myself a homeless person for quite some time. Terrifying only when I think of it. Also exciting because I have been blessed with tools to help myself. Will just have to see what happens next. Next...I take a good look at these jail walls, sometimes I find

them as an essential novel. I'm telling you, these jail walls definitely has a story to tell. Other's blood and guts in jail are left on these walls to help me write my novel. Strange isn't it? Guided by the imminent dead. Few hours have passed and absolutely everything is the same. What's not the same is the weather. Just took a knack out the widow... dreadful weather is happening now. Full blast of rain and it comes with small particles of ice. Never seen this before. Back in the cell is even more bad news. The wind blew all the rain in my cell and it happens to have a wet floor. I guess it's just the usual shit day. It's fine. This is how it works in jail. One sunny day. One shitty day. I'm just not going to care anymore. Whatever the jail brings on me I'll take it. Scorpions, snakes, bed bugs, dog food. Anything. I can take it. 32 more days and I'm out. One last thing for today...Long ago I've been told by a successful writer that "time" is what must be sacrificed for anything successful to happen. It better be worth it for I spent 100 days in jail eating dog food and that's not okay. Although I still don't know what success has to do with dog food. I know, I know. I'm just a clown who's feeling down, except that I don't have clown shit to look like one. I have dog food instead. Howl, howl.

15. 1. 2020: Violent wind all day. This whether it kills my creativity. Sometimes the wind blows the rain into my cell and it goes all over my papers. My table is located just opposite the window. I like to call it my writing table although is just another jail table. On a good day when the weather is alright I get a blow of sun and this blow it warms up my jail table, by the way, it's made from rusty cold iron and it feel shit when I write on it. On a sunny day it feels alright.

Don't ask me why, that's just how it is. I'm not sure if I told you about my window. Much of the window is missing, it got broken the other day. Had to take it all out, the frame included. Don't worry, I can't escape. There's another layer of security, jail bars made vertical like most jails has. What's really good is that on a windy day when blows of wind gets into my cell it cleans up the toilet smell. Not actually a bad thing. When I get out I will probably remember for a very long time this ugly jail smell and I will remember it so vividly. This horrid smell. This horrid cell. This horrid jail. Lingering on me... disgusting smell. Oh boy...it's so freaking cold today in my cell. It feels like I got naked in the snow and there's no clothes to put on. Never going back to jail. Lessons scar, like bicycle training scar. 100 days is enough to scar the blood out of me. Already night time and I'm thinking to go to bed. Winter days are short. There is something rather annoying about going to bed around 5:00p.m. I could do something creative. Anything really. But what else you can do in jail but just eat, shit, take a piss and sleep. At home I was working on my music until 3:00a.m, then, sleep for a couple of hours and get back to something even more creative. DJ for a few hours, going thru my vinyl collection, sample a few sounds, make a song, check the clubs, always creative stuff. Always excited to stay awake. Create. Create. Create. In jail...sleep, eat shit...shit, shit, shit. Actually there's not much to shit from me. These days jail food it comes with a budget on my tray. On a good day I get the dog food, on a bad day I get the egg. And it's fuckin off always. Smells so bad. Oh...I feel like want to vomit only when think of jail food. The toilet started to burst again and I can't do anything. Going to sleep with shit smell on my nose. Definitely clown shit.

16. 1. 2020: Just woke up. Can't believe I slept all night and all afternoon. Went to sleep in the night time, woke up in the night time. I stayed in bed for so long intentionally so I can forget about the smell that comes from the toilet. Can't believe I sleep with the toilet half a meter from me. Well...maybe just over a meter but is still too closer to my bed. Only an alien would want to sleep with a toilet near his bed. Sometimes I get to see burps of gasses coming out of it and it gets released in the air. When that happens my cell becomes an

almost gas chamber. Thank God I have a window to escape for air. Sometimes I think is a great idea to have a broken window. I get plenty of air. Can't actually close it because is missing. The other day I took out the whole frame. It just came off because it was old. A few days later the jail guard asked me where's the window, I told him it just disappeared in the middle of the night and when I said that I actually pretended I catch butterflies so i can be left alone. He eventually closed the cell and said nothing. I'm in crazy peoples place so I better look like one to be left alone. So yes, I look out the window, I do some writing and try to get along with most things that I don't like including the smell of this cell which I totally hate. Doing my time, pretend I am crazy, and hopefully in a few days I get out alive and sane. It sounds like a plan. Yesterday when went to sleep I crept myself over the mattress but I done it carefully to avoid disturbing the bed bugs. God damn bedbugs are all over the place in this cell. Bedbugs heaven. They're all waiting to suck the life out of me. Going to sleep it will be my worst memory from jail. I have not seen that many bed bugs since my time at Bayswater hostel. Let me tell you all about it. It's a cheep London hostel just opposite Nothing Hill market. Now that I mentioned its name I'm afraid I've been hit by some very bad memories coming straight from that place. It was around that area once I got mugged by a bunch of thieves. Happened in the dead of December 2009. Just came back from my awful job….I was washing pots at Gaucho restaurant just opposite Piccadilly Circus which is in the heart of London. If I remember correctly I finished my shift around 3:30a.m. That night it was someone's birthday. Someone famous. The restaurant was filed with celebrities, actors, musicians, entrepreneurs. Londoners love a good night out. Don't worry...I was completely invisible to everyone. I mean c'mon, who gives a fuck for a five foot pot washer, wearing kitchen apron, a cap, washing-up gloves, goggles and farm boots. Another pot washer probably. I finish my shift and took the road towards the Nothing Hill Gate. Crossed the London Bridge and head straight for the hostel. I actually preferred long walks in the middle of the night. London looks cool at night. At the hostel I was sleeping in a bunk bed. Sharing the room with others was something I never enjoy doing it but back in 2009 I was very poor, doing crap jobs and sometimes going from job to job and couldn't afford more than just a bunk bed and a buss ticket to work and my way back. I arrived in Bayswater around 5.30 a.m. Still very dark outside. Nights are long in the winter. I took the Bayswater road to cut a mile in half. So many times I took that shortcut but that night it appeared to be bad luck. Got mugged. Suddenly I see these two geezas jumping in front of me, both wearing black masks. I did not even seen them coming. In two seconds I think I received a dozen punches. Felt on the ground and they start checking my pockets, my bag, around my neck and my hands too. I think they were looking for gold chains, rings or something. Possibly an expensive watch. But for a pot washer that's not something I use to have. My most valuable possessions on me were a couple of books and my ipod. I had no other valuables. Payday supposed to be the next day. I usually got paid in my bank account and never cash in hand. But these motherfuckers got so angry because they couldn't find anything on me. One of them took his dick out and pissed on me. He pissed on my head first then he would move his dick left and right and he would do it slowly to get as much piss all over me. The other one spit on me. I felt totally deprived of any human qualities. Felt totally dehumanised. But for a bunch of criminals this must be a fun night out. Police came and I don't even know how they found me. I think someone seen what happened and report it. They came quick. I remember one police officer approached me to take a statement from me. It was a woman police officer. She was standing right there in front of me doing police work, asking all kind of questions which I did responded, and as I was trying to explain as clearly as possible she took some distance from me. She eventually asked me what was with the smell on me. It was that motherfucker that took a piss on me. I was smelling very badly of urine. Minutes later they told me to come with them at the police station to take samples of DNA from my clothing. It appeared this smart police work end up successful. A week later I was called back at the station and told they managed to find those who attacked me but thanks to the DNA match. I remember being invited in one of those police rooms where they interview criminals and they had this window that looked like a mirror on one side and normal on the other side. Basically the person who is interviewed cant see who's behind the window. On the other side were a few men. They've been all asked for telling their names loud and I immediately recognised the ones who punched me. It was their voice that I immediately recognised. When I took a good look at their faces...oh my. They looked so unapologetically criminals. Both got five years each in jail. But they were also wanted for other crimes and their jail sentence went up to 12 years each. What a story and is more like a dozen years old. I could probably write and re-write "Blood And Guts In Jail" with these type of stories all day long. The amount of shit — life threw on me is unbelievable. There's a spark of sun in my cell. How cool is that. It's already morning. Cool little sunrise happens just now. I wish you could see it. Small blow of sun goes all over my arms. Loving this warm blow. Winter'ish but works well. Going to sleep. Nothing else to do. Boring...

17. 1. 2020: Oh...how horrible. Woke up with burping noises coming from the toilet and the God damn toilet is near my bed. Awful. There's shit smell all over. 29 more days to go and I'm out from this gas chamber. It kinda feels like.

18. 1. 2020: Afternoon raining on-and-off. Sea looking calmer today. Not much wind. A few birds came by my window, they look like seagulls. Couldn't give them any food for I'm as poor as a church mouse. These days I barely have any food for me. Today I had the usual bowl of slop. Oh...horrible. Even more horrible when I think I have to eat that crap for the next 28 days. I can see a couple of fishing boats in the pier. I think they're unloading fish...I think. Some construction workers too. Quite a lot of activity today. The view from my window is alright. Glad I see some human activity. But still struggling with the toilet smell. The problem is not the toilet, the problem is my attitude about the smell. I just can't stop hating that smell. When I look out the window, It's contagious, It will either warm my heart or it gives me an instant mood lift. When I look back in the cell is more like I look into a pigs ass and smell it in the same time. Everything else is murder. Ugly fuckin jail smell....and is everywhere. There's a woodpecker drumming at my window. I'm so hungry that I might eat him alive. Feeling incredibly boring today. Not sure what to do next. Wait, I have a great idea, let's just sit back and wait until I get out of jail. Like there's something else better to be done but just waiting for time to pass me by. What a brilliant idea. And maybe also try hit my head against the wall until I get out of jail. Wouldn't be even better to hit my head so hard that I'll go to sleep for 28 days.

Wake up an hour before I get out. That will be something. Seriously, I sometimes have a strange feeling that I'm in a dream, but this dream is more like one of those Big Brother episodes and as much as I want to wake up I can't. I'm trapped into one ugly episode. Maybe I'm on some sleeping pills and I can't wake up from them. Actually It feels like I'm on many things. It's probably the jail smell playing clown shit with me. Bunch of birds flying on-and-off around my head right now. They're small birds the size of a coin and are all yellow and looks very animated. There's ten of them now. Wait...one more just popped. How on earth these birds went inside my cell? Am I really dreaming or I gone nuts? I'm curious what's in those birds heads? Because my view of the birds brain especially those flying around my head will be different from how my brain works. Actually everything is just ghosting appearances. Slippery and hard to pin down birds all disappeared. Definitely they put something in my food. Motherfuckers. They are trying to shut me down. My vision is unclear. I feel tired. Actually I feel dizzy. I need to rest. Sending this cable to my girl just in case I die.

...e-mail a prisoner. Copy...saint Isaac, cell 13

Dear Julia,

...my-sweet-caramel-candy-girl, Papa Saint Isaac sends you kisses and hopes you're not too sad. If I die please bring your Spotify playlist at my funeral. Kiss you lovingly and remain your true mystery lover. Good night you fuckin bitch.

..e-mail a prisoner. Copy...Julia to cell 13...

...wait, what songs you want me to add to your playlist?

Yours, Julia

19. 1. 2020: I'm alive but woke up with terrible pain on my back. The bed got bent right in the middle. It just collapsed but I don't see that as worth fixing. 26 more days and I'm getting the fuck outta here. Oh...my back...It hurts so bad. Some rain during the day. This time outside not in my cell, although, sometimes, a blow of wind it brings all the rain into my cell. Most times it depends how the wind blows. If

it blows from the north then I get the full blow right outside my window and since I don't have a window it's like death by a thousand cuts. It happens all the times. Usually once or twice a day I get the full blow. In the night-time is the worst. Feels like ghosts coming by my cell. I imagine all kind of strange things. I even imagined a vampire standing by my window and looking at me at all times. It's green and has large teeth. Just like the front cover of my book. Something like that. Must be the author creating a bunch of strange dreams especially for me. Oh poor me for I'm as poor as a church mouse. At least I have dreams to hope for. Saw a bird coming by my window. I think it was a woodpecker. It didn't bother to make a hole in the wall so I can get out of here. Oh my days for I'm as bored as a couch potato. What else can I do but just wait, wait, wait. Wait to get out. Horrible life in jail. Ridiculous bullshit low life, sitting in bed all day and all night and staring at the wall in front of me. I think I become the wall. Sometimes when I stare at the wall for quite some time I can see my shadow slowly moving to the left. It does that because of the sun position. In the morning, my shadow tends to be exactly in front of me. As the sun slowly makes its way toward the sunset, my shadow too moves with the sun and I stand still looking at it. Looking at my own shadow like a freak. Like a creep. Like a bum-sucker. It never talks to me this shadow. It is always mute. Maybe is because I stayed too much in one place...now I become the place. Back home I was always doing something creative. One hour in the book room doing some writing, two hours later doing some reading, then head in the music studio, doing some songwriting. Sometimes even going for a run in the middle of the night. I miss running at night. Especially running with my ipod in my hand and listening to some of my favourite music. I tend to listen quite a lot of pop house. I told you the story with the London job....the pot washing job. After work I was doing these long walks in the middle of the night, just me with my iPod in my hand. But let's forget the part when I got mugged and pissed all over in the middle of the night. I hated that job but I loved my London walks. In the middle of the night of course. After work, It was all about me and London. I think I stayed in that job for one year just to enjoy these walks at night. I miss those times. Less the pot washing. But I won't wash pots again when I get out of jail. I'm thinking of becoming windswept and interesting until somebody will tell me I am quite interesting. After that I simply have to maintain my reputation then people will notice that I am one and once they accept it — and pronounced that I am an interesting person — I'm all set. I then have to hang out with only windswept and interesting people so we can recognise echoers because we all have one thing in common...a bunch of capitalist assholes, our own cute little version of financialization. How sweet — now windswept and interesting people can become little capitalist assholes. Gosh...all I wish now is to look for a sucker to buy my NFT's. I guess when I get out of jail it would be easy for me to bank a seven figure number by turning this existential crisis into a string of 1000 numbered NFTs. Convinced this is the best idea that came to my mind since sliced bread. The problem is jail bread tends to suck but I'll still spend decades making art. I'm so bored. Need to do something. Probably count the bed bugs. Going to send a cable to Julia.

...e-mail a prisoner. Copy...saint Isaac, cell 13

"Dear Julia,

You know something girl...I'm crazy for you. What if I tell you right now I'm a slow mover around you, walk in sexy pace with my jail pyjamas on, and I hold the keys to a happy life with you.

..e-mail a prisoner. Copy...Julia to cell 13...

Wha? Ya drunk or something? I'm already happy ya wee pocket monkey! Say something different. Tell me how beautiful I am. And I also want you to tell me I'm hot and you like ma sexy smile. Understand? And you're definitely on the cunt path.

...e-mail a prisoner. Copy...saint Isaac, cell 13

Girl, try to relax, right now I'm using my deepest-sounding voice. Can you try set the mood for both of us and imagine you're establishing some closeness with me?

..e-mail a prisoner. Copy...Julia to cell 13...

Wha? Ya drunk or something? Ya stink. And ya got the bed bugs. Tell me something nice, I want to feel special. I'm rich girl. Understand?

...e-mail a prisoner. Copy...saint Isaac, cell 13

Julia my girl, If we were together right now I'd run my fingers under your arms and give you a row of tickles and I'll do that slowly in the same time I kiss you. Does that makes you feel special?

..e-mail a prisoner. Copy...Julia to cell 13...

Yer drunk or something? Ya need grabbing my cunt every chance ya get. Understand? Otherwise I'll dump ya. Fuck off!

20. 1. 2020: Woke up with a terrible cold in my body. I never felt so much cold in my entire life. Starting to have these body tremors and are uncontrollable. It happens all over my body, particularly in the legs. When I stand up and try walk for a little I can see my legs shaking and can't do anything. What was randomly now has

become constantly. God help me get out alive from this hell for I really want to still enjoy some life on the outside. I once read in a book that life can be short. I hope mine is long enough to still have time to write a second book. Found block of ice under my sink. It appears the cold messed-up the pipe. I still have running water but it comes at a low pressure. During the day rain on-and-off. Sometimes snow, sometimes rain, sometimes rain and snow. Very strange weather. Earlier today a full blast of wind hit my missing window and minutes later rain all over. End up with water all over my papers. It also came with some small particles of ice. I thought is from another planet this type of weather. Could barely keep up with the window. Had to cover it with the only blanket I have then blanket got wet. Right now I'm in a disparate need for a dry blanket. In the evening the rain reasonably stoped a little but still spritzing here and there. No snow. Looking at the night sky I have the impression is Christmas. I know Christmas passed a while a go but there's something strange about the alignment of stars, in particular one bright star that just appeared in the eastern sky. It looks just like the star of Bethlehem. Hopefully it's a sign from God I get out alive. Nothing else to do but just force myself to go to sleep covered by a wet blanket. I could probably try to portray the perfect killer sky by looking at the star of Bethlehem and tell myself...or tell Jesus..."oh Jesus...I wish you could see this...lights comes up...your star just got born...I never seen a paint that captures the beauty of the night in a moment like this." I better shut-up otherwise is bad news for my jail life. Might have to remember this on a cruise when I transit the Atlantic. Hopefully I get a sky like this. Hocus-pocus-preparatus it's time to go to sleep. Abracadabra works.

21. 1. 2020: It took me nearly three months to realise keeping a diary in jail is moral boosting to a prisoner. It could be like an old friend. Let's just call it an imaginary friend. This imaginary friend never talks. Never asks you for something. It just sits there on the table waiting for you to pick up your pen and write about this old friend....an imaginary friend. I believe this old friend can guide you live a creative life in jail. Something to do until your liberation day. Just saying...in case one day you get the jail. Today I came to the conclusion that it happen to the best of us. All kind of shit can happen to the best of us. Right now in this very moment you might decide to go for a drive. You take your keys. You start the engine. You pop the music loud and think about your best date. You might even think about getting a drink. Pop a molly under your lip and two minutes and thirty seven seconds later you hit a cyclist. Eight minutes and twelve seconds later police came and you've been arrested for...for god knows what. Another twenty five minutes and ten seconds later you're in your worst nightmare....you talk with a lawyer to give you the best possible options...this is something called legal advice. One hour and twenty minutes later you face a judge. Four hours and nine minutes later you've been found guilty and sentenced to two years in jail...or ten years in jail? Hopefully it will only be a home arrest. I'm only telling you to keep an open mind... anyone can get the jail. Including me. Well...I kinda got it. But one could suck at driving but still get the jail. One could also sucks at writing but have faith to survive in a jail. If you ever arrive in these places keep a healthy diary and look forward to your liberation day. Got to go now. My meal just arrived. The usual...shit. It kinda makes me sick.

22. 1. 2020: Eat + Sleep + Think + Write + Repeat = Jail Life. Tried and tested. I just finish cleaning my cell. Plenty of crap all over the place especially on the floor. Well…I only have the floor…this ain't a luxury hotel, it's a cell. It's called Crispy Bacon Motel. No TV. No balcony. No fancy furniture but just a chair and a table. Dirty. Ugly. Miserable fuckin cell. I hate it. If I hate it my readers can too. For the past two months I've been throwing food on the floor and I done it intentionally just because I hate the jail food. Sometimes I thought that if I throw it on the floor they'll give me better food. I was wrong. They gave me dog food. And sometimes I would do it because I'm angry and sometimes because I'm hungry. But most times I do it because I hate this jail. Now the cell is tidy. I've been using my hands as a brush to clean the floor and it actually worked out. But no matter how much I try to clean the cell it's never enough, the smell is still there…oh gosh it smells so bad. Filthy. Ugly. Smelly cell. I just can't get the jail smell out. Let me describe it to you because every day it changes. It's like a god damn chameleon this jail smell. Generally it smells like a cross between body odour… imagine you haven't got a wash for like three months or something. Well…more like me. I stink these days but once I get out definitely getting the bath. Another layer of smell found in my cell or layers I shall say…will be stale air, cleaning supplies…something like chlorine or bleach, old lady soap, expired spicy foods and occasionally farts. But farts from an old man that just had a Chinese take away. Depending on who your celly or neighbour is can greatly impact what you smell. I'm alone. Myself and every piece of stone found in this cell. Good company I guess. Beautiful sunset happening right now. Been awake for most of the day and the previous night. Done

some reading, quite a bit of writing, some cleaning and here I am now...another day in jail passed by. For me this is the most amazing piece of news at the end of the day. But I find it stupid to wish your days runs out more faster. Life is short and our days are numbered but in jail is the price you pay. I wish you could see it...lights comes down...the sun slowly goes away...I never seen a paint that captures the beauty of the evening on a moment like this. Surprisingly amazing sunset moment for a winter. And it also reflects in the snow, making it a blue'ish like colour here and there. Hopefully next time I will experience the whole thing from the corner of a sunny beach. But there's other things that happens in my life and it concerns me. At least for the past few days. Recently I start noticing some unusual pain also some pressure in the left side of my head and it happens only when I get very upset. This pain it also makes me very depressed. When It happens I behave very unusual and I do it without knowing much what I'm doing or what I'm saying. As a result I may find it difficult to communicate...well, the only communication goes between me and my diary. Sometimes my behaviour is erratic. I don't think I'm rude or awkward. It's just this unusual pain that creates everything. Or at least most of it. I really don't know what's happening with me. I'm just afraid of being sick of something and I can tell you...being sick in jail is bad news. No one gives a fuck if anything happens to you. It's pretty much game over if a serious health condition takes over you. But maybe I'm fine. Maybe is just a moment in my life that makes me feel this way... which kinda is. I'm looking at my jail table. A very ugly table made from rusty old metal. Very uncomfortable table to write on it... probably that's why my writing is so uncomfortable...it sucks and is all over the place…it's because of the table. I'd rather go write on the floor. Rather depressive to look at this table. There's not much on it but just plain dust, my diary, and a plastic bowl that I use for meals. I haven't washed my bowl for the past two months. I know is not hygienic but who cares…I'm in jail. There's also a plastic spoon, a plastic fork and a plastic cup. None washed. I know, I know…they're all dirty but will leave them that way for the next 23 days. Is when I get out. My hands are also dirty…they look like I just came back from a mining job. Dirt under my nails. Black dirt. My nails hasn't been cut since…since I left home for jail. I haven't told anyone just yet but before I left home for my court date and then sent to jail, I had this long bath, and it was more like spending half the day in the god damn bathroom. Like I knew I'll get the jail. What can I say…It was a good bath indeed. I miss a hot bath. I miss my body cream, my shampoo, my after shave, my toothpaste. Oh…for fuck sake…the toothpaste…I better don't say anything about toothpaste. My mouth stinks. Not okay to not wash your teeth for almost three months. You know what? I'm tired. Been awake all night. Some bugs on the floor. Whatsoever. Don't care. It's part of the jail life. Beautiful sunrise by the way. Calm sea. Going to bed with this marvellous image of nature. If I don't wake up I presume I'll be dead and cremated at sea. Man…this is nonsense. Can't believe I'm going to bed with such ugly thoughts. Excruciating these last few days.

23. 1. 2020: I have just finished with doing a bit more cleaning. This time the toilet. There was crap all over the place. Around the wall and a little on the floor. For the past few days the toilet is

making a burp and when that happens it brings crap on the surface. Anything that is stuck on the pipe. Sometimes I even get others shit into my toilet. Depending how strong the burp is crap goes on the floor and sometimes on the wall. I think is caused by excess air. I get to hear these random nosies...like someone's farts. Horrible. Yet this is real jail life. Gotta get used to this shit for the next 22 days. Today I striped-down from all my clothes so I can take a good look on my body. I was terrified what I seen. My legs are so skinny, barely any muscle left, just bones covered by a thin layer of skin. My ribs are very much visible...arms are just skin and bones. Very happy I don't have a mirror to see myself a living skeleton. If I keep going with my water diet I might put a few grams of skin on me. Gotta keep up with those skin layers. It's all I have...skin & layers and a shitty skeleton. Lost almost half of my body weight but alive. A beautiful and rainy evening with as much as possible rain showing into my cell. Delighted. I swear on her majesty cedar soap that all my life I wanted a moment like this. I'm just going to take a seat on this cold & ugly chair and write about the colours of my walls. They're all white anyway. Boring plain white. The colour of hungry, loneliness and insanity. I hate colour white.

24.1.2020: Woke up with a brilliant idea. It came to me while I was sleeping. I have decided that during my lifetime I will very much want to win an award for my writing. A book prize. Any type of award will do. I hope I win something. My favourite one will be the award for a low-down story in a velvet bag. If that won't work and it proves that this book will be a total waste in the history of literature then I'll make YouTube videos on how to apply makeup step-by-step, and I'll also play some fuckin bullshit comedy on a children's radio and show live how to fill a glass of water from the kitchen sink. But don't forget about the McDonald's mini happy meal complete toy food maker, I'll probably play with that shit too. Seems ingenious don't you think? Complete jail plan. Let me put this into my diary. It is important for me to have brilliant ideas when I get out. Also to remember them. I'm also thinking to sell some flavoured water. It will make me rich. You don't believe me? Read a book by the name of "Blood And Guts in Jail" but try keep an open mind because today I'm on vitamins. Motherfuckers, they drugged me again. For some reason the sunset is marmalade cedar pink. Raining this evening but cleared-up just before a blow of asteroids. They came in small particles of dust. It's great to see an asteroid from my window. For some reason it got stuck in the air. My hands are looking exceptionally well. I like my nails. Rest assured it will make a good impression to my girl. Sea calmer. A few dolphins are smiling at me. For the first time since I arrived in jail I feel totally okay. It's the dolphins. Actually the medicine they gave me. I don't know.

25. I. 2020: I keep write random words that leads to sentences, then sentences to paragraphs and paragraphs to chapters. There's no order nor sanity but just chaos and insanity. Everyday is exactly the same. Draconian long distance custody, it feels like never liberating, always a painful memory. Fuck these vampires...I just received a blow from a couple of jail guards. Both came into my cell and being told today's food it will be suspended due to rough

weather. Apparently the food supply run into difficulties. It looks like someone is experiencing problems with delivery and it might take a few days to arrive. Until then I will be on a one-egg-a-day diet and for breakfast I shall have a glass of water. Dinner will be a good read from the local newspaper. I've been told there are quite a few good pictures to stimulate my imagination. In particularly pictures with seagulls and guillemots working together to fish. It's great! This is really good! Local postcards for dinner. Man, fuck this. This is bullshit low life living. Fuck this jail. I look like a thin carrot and expect to lose more weight for the next 20 days. And when I get out I look like shit but my passion for writing it will prove an instant hit. I don't even know how that came to me. Probably it came with the wind. Let me put this one into my diary. It is important for me to remember one who flew over the cuckoo's nest it happens to look like me. One brilliant idea into my nest. Awesome! I think we can both agree I'm still not awake from yesterday's medicine. Shod just try completely forget about food and go straight to bed. First thing I will do when I wake up tomorrow is think about a nice holiday and a new pair of teeth to the tune of at least £50,000. My teeth like those of all whose been to jail and most addicts are all totally fucked-up and the only way to get my confidence back is to get a new set of sparkling white teeth. Like the ones from Netflix. I think we can both agree I'm still not awake from yesterday's medicine and absolutely everything I say is not me. Better shut-up and gently go to sleep.

26. 1. 2020: Another day goes by and I don't understand the reasons why everything is exactly the same. Walls are the same… plain boring white, oh God, I hate them. Food is the same. Today I had the usual egg and it made my stomach churn. I then spent most of the day on the toilet. What's not the same is the weather. Looking out the window I can see a beautiful blue sky. Yesterday ugly as an old man ass, today bright and colourful like Alice in Wonderland. It seems to me the weather is very strange in these parts of the world. Maybe is indeed a stranger part of wonderland. Let me count my Humpty Dumpty eggs. The original Humpty Dumpty egg is missing because I'm looking for a change in life. Here we go again while I am alive. Everyday I find myself in these pages and is more like a meeting with myself. The more I write about my life in jail the more is about my life on the outside and very little about the book itself. Maybe is because right now I'm at home in my bedroom, trapped in an imaginary world where I can spit it all out otherwise this book it would never be complete. For the first time my life is validated and complete. There you go, the author told the truth. Finally. Back in jail is bad news. Today I have decided to wear a face mask. It stinks like thick mud. Something spectacular happened while I was sleeping. The toilet burped and shit got out but since by nature I'm a man of many talents I just used my hands to clean the shit out of it and I even had a happy meal with my hands unwashed. Off eggs on the menu. Well, in jail this is my only menu. Recently I start taking a note of how many meals I had in jail. I have them all written here. As far as I remember I had 80 off-eggs, 80 slices of mouldy bread and sometimes it came with spider eggs between the slices. Fuck…they are salty and it doesn't taste too good. I was talking about the

spider eggs. Not to forget about the slop but they call it jail soup. This shit is pure alien blood and it also made my urine go green. Somedays my urine will go yellow, then red, blue and green again. Last week I felt like a traffic light waiting at the cubicle. I nearly forgot about the dog food. Motherfuckers, they feed me with dog food so many times and I didn't know what I was eating. It's fuckin hilarious. In total I had 48 cans of dog poo. Sorry, I mean dog food. Oh god...yuck. Gross. Disgusting. Totally unappetising. But there were also good days and these are rare days when I had something alright. Full size bread, block of butter, pack of biscuits and sloppy sauce with jail water. These were the hospitals days. Told you I've been in hospital for a week. Today's food was no good. One slice of bread and the usual slop. Better stop thinking about food. Nice evening with clear sky. The sunset is making the sky look a little orange towards the horizon. Beautiful. Sea calmed down. Not much wind. Lights off. Going to sleep. Nothing else to do.

27.1.2020: Today I've been staring at a blank piece of paper until my forehead started to bleed. I just can't write anything. Nothing comes out. There are days — and these are legendary days, when I write in my diary without interruption, everything it just flows. And there are days like these... as if as someone remotely set me on the uninteresting mode, and everything I try to write down has no prospect of progress or success or a stretch of road between nowhere and somewhere. I know, I know, it doesn't make any sense. I sometimes tend to think that trying to write a book is a total waste of time. Hoping to make my diary into a book? That must be some kind of achievement. Are you thinking what I'm thinking? But don't get the jail, instead, take the first left, walk until the clock strikes midnight and look for the Crispy Bacon Motel. Don't ask me for directions, instead, use your imagination, capture someone's attention, jump three feet, whistle, drink, and be merry, then, check-in and organise the estate of a mysterious manuscript. I'm assuming something it will quickly turn into some kind of script. And they also have better tables to write your thing. I just want to take a sit and calm down. Bullshit low life, in jail your mind feels like a whirlwind. Right now all I want to imagine is my last job as a cleaner. I remember very well this lady in a higher level of management and everything in her office was pink, computer mouse was pink, pink pen, even pink hair. I say this to try forget about these ugly white walls in my cell. Why must jails have white walls? I can't put it into words. And why bother put it into words. Oh, I hate my chair. It's all rusty cold iron. Absolutely wretched fuckin chair. It sucks the life out of me. I wish I could have a better chair. It's so quiet in my cell. Not even a sound. Total silence. Jail food just arrived. I better keep up with the dog food...it makes my stomach run smooth. Gosh, I need something to stimulate my imagination even if is complete fake news.

28. 1. 2020: Woke up again with toilet burps. This time the noise was so loud that I thought I had a drunk man into my cell and did not knew he is keeping me company. I usually sleep facing the wall because it's too ugly to see my cell. Sometimes it's frightening to open my eyes and see what I'm looking at...one ugly cell. Totally boring. Never a feeling of happiness. Always making me feel

depressed. So I prefer to keep my eyes closed. Oh…for fuck sake…
there's a ton of ugly smell into my cell. Water all over the floor and
shit flows freely. The water is coming from the toilet. About an inch
of water already. Small pieces of shit are floating all over the place.
Dead rat in the corner. The rat apparently came out from the toilet.
It appears to be dead. I think he drowned himself. I don't even care.
What I care is my time. Instead of writing…or perhaps relax my mind
with a few hours of staring out the window but not to find out what
is going on outside because is not much but just a bunch of hills, the
sea and birds flying nowhere but to exercise in discovering the
contents of my own mind, because my mind is fucked-up since I got
the jail, and it also appears to be a sunny day outside and sunny
days are rare in this part of the world, I wasted all day cleaning my
cell. I had to get rid of the floating shit and the rat of course and I
done it just by using my hands. No gloves. Just hands. I had no soap
at all to wash my hands afterwards. Only plain cold water. I can tell
you that my hands smells shit. I'm in jail so It really doesn't matter.
But these last few days have now become excruciating. 17 days are
like months away. It just feels that way. Anyway, some good news
today. After cleaning my cell got letter from the governor saying he
is pleased to inform me that my release is considered accordingly
with the end date of my sentence. It says he has no plans to keep
me longer than my sentence. Apparently I behaved. Or maybe they
just run out of dog food and wants to get rid of me. I really don't
care, in a few days I'm out and return to my life on the outside, write
a second book, travel the world, make music, go for my artist career
because I'm so much behind with everything and I will even dare to
do some more. More? More in my next book. The letter is also

saying that my property which is basic stuff like, well...the stuff I left home for jail, whatever was on me...I nearly forgot, are ready to be picked-up from the prison reception on the day of my release. Signed, the governor. He put his own name. Mr Chris Fraser. The news are good. Best news in 100 days. Looking at the bottom of the letter it says that I need to provide them an address for their records. It looks like they wanna put me on probation for the first 60 days and it starts from the 1st day when I'm out. It's called parole. There are certain behavioural conditions, including checking-in with their designated parole officers or else they may rearrest me and returned to prison. But I'm too pretty to go back to jail. I don't even plan to return. I'll just give them the address from the shop around the corner. I'm homeless anyway. Don't have an address. In the first 24 hours of my release I will probably be as far as man can ever walk on barefoot earth. Better to live in a tent somewhere in a forest than in this cell along with the bed bugs, termites, and God knows whatever is around me. Strange things happens around this cell. At least I will be free, make a fire, hunt a few rabbits because mother nature always have something for someone like me, and backpack the shit out of my boots. I have big plans for "Blood And Guts Before I Die." That will be all for today. It took me a day and a night to actually write something into my diary. I write for a minute, then, I take a short walk wall to wall and I do it for at least an hour, in the same time I'm thinking what to write next. But I'm also thinking to a thousand more useless shit. Stuff that fogs my head. It's called brain fog. In the dictionary it says that it isn't actually a medical condition, but rather a term used to describe the feeling of being mentally sluggish and fuzzy. In jail, brain fog can impact the way you feel about yourself. Look at me, I feel like a useless piece of shit. Most times I don't even know what shod I think of...I guess I mostly think of useless boring shit. Blame the winter for is like an unhappy episode of the past. This cold is a scandal that never stops. I swear it's sunrise now. Here it comes...lights on. Time for me to snooze off to sleep before too much light. The real Saint Isaac was a vampire. Watch out. Wish I can have a Google Assistant to tell him "lights out."

29. 1. 2020: I couldn't sleep. Woke up as often as every ten minutes. I stand. I walk. I sit down. I stand. I walk. I sit down. It's hilarious how small this cell is. A proper cubicle the size of a public toilet. Wish I could have a larger place to at least walk around for a bit. It will also do me good. These days my legs are fucked. I fear of loss of bone from inactivity, always bound to a bed. Usually a patient or someone who has become very ill and is no longer able to move easily is confined to their bed. I kinda feel that way. Seriously annoying. I received my food and it's a joke. One potato. Not even proper cooked. Half boiled, half raw. This jail sucks. I closed my eyes and pretend I like it. It tasted horrible. I chuck the rest of it in the toilet. At least half of it. For a moment I imagined eating a chunk of poo. I'm looking out the window to see what's happening outside. Beautiful afternoon. Sunny & clean, almost no wind. But very cold. Strange looking bird keeps coming back to my window. This one it's the size of a swan. All white. Has large wings, long legs, a very long bony mouth. Seems to be one of those fishing birds. It comes by my window, takes a good look inside and goes away. Sometimes is staring at me like she wants to communicate with me or something. I have no fish for sale today. Poor as a church mouse, is who I am. She probably thinks I'm a mouse. Gave this bird a name, Leila. Don't know why. It's the only name it came to my mind. One day I will probably draw this bird on a pice of paper and show it to the whole world. It was my only friend in jail. A bird. Oh gosh, I go insane these last two weeks and I'm not even a former prisoner with many years of experience. I know, I know. I'm just a clown who's feeling down, except that I don't have clown shit to look like one. Last night I was laying in bed and I was thinking about the lifers kept here. I just can't

imagine how terrible can be to be kept in this fuckin place for a lifetime. Jesus Christ. Must be a nightmare. In two weeks I'm out. By the way, "lifer" is a term used for a prisoner serving a whole life sentence. Terrifying, don't you think?...serving a whole life sentence you can expect a whole life of horrors behind bars. I think is life after death for a prisoner who serves a whole life tariff. Kept in a cell for the whole life. I think It doesn't really strike you until later that you are never going to get out. It plants a seed of depression in your brain that for the rest of your life you are going to be getting up every morning and seeing the same brick of walls in front of you and knowing that wall is all you are going to see for the rest of your days. And that is K.O. You are never going to see a tree again or most probably the people who you love. When the reality hits you that you are never ever going to walk on the street, see a tree, get on a bus, drive a car, all the little things we're taking for granted, i imagine you'll be quite suicidal. I only been in this jail for nearly three months and I definitely felt that way at least a hundred times. Can't imagine being here a whole life. I would probably put an end to my days just because of the idea of belonging to a jail for the rest of my life...is just terrifying. Going to bed. Sorry, I'm scared of these terrifying thoughts. I need to clam down. Will try to get some rest, hopefully it will help.

30.1.2020: Wish I could be somewhere in the Fiji islands resting under a palm tree and sipping coconut water out of a coconut. The truth is that I'm very much in jail holding a plastic cup filed with jail water. Maybe another time coconut water. Today is a very sunny day outside and I'm stuck in jail. It kills me when I think of it. I shod be standing one feet high docked in a hammock and facing the sea. Yeah, yeah, yeah...bullshit, bullshit, bullshit. I wish. Prison diaries looks alright, so far I managed to write about a thousand pages and at least a quarter of them it will go into the book. The rest of it I will probably sell them as original works of art. Something like NFT's, which stands for non fungible capitalist asshole, but in the metaverse they call it a token. I bet someone will pay at least an ether for my toilet paper. Did I told you I used actual toilet paper to write most of the book? Now you know what you paid for. But you get the story so thats a proper bonus. So far I think I have like 50 meters of toilet paper hidden under the bed. At least two dozen pages went inside the book using the material I wrote on toilet paper. Oh my jail days for I'm so lonely, sad, depressed, sick, and drunk from too much jail water. I hate that water. It taste like shit. Every time I drink a cup of jail water it's more like I try to poison myself. Yet still alive and full hands on the manuscript. I still have flashbacks...sometimes nightmares...hearing the judge..."You are remanded into custody." Two minutes later put inside a prisoner transport van and drove me straight to jail. Half way I came by air. Actually I don't even know where in the hell I am. Definitely on an island...is all I know. Well, thats what happens when you are remanded into custody. Straight to jail. But there was more. The journey took nearly six hours and those hours were only worries in my head, thinking how I could manage for the next 100 days. And you could imagine how worried I was...I was waiting in that jail van, not knowing where I will be sent, all I know is I was soaked in sweat and worries. You hear all these stories about prison, it's not the actual fear of prison it's the fear of not knowing.

Thats what you have to overcome. Six hours later I finally arrived at the prison and the wait in the van seemed like hours, sweat running down my forehead, fearing what was to come. Finally I was taken in. I filled through to reception then on to a side room for a strip-search and the strip-search it includes checking your asshole. Yes people, you heard that, someone made me bend and even told me to relax my asshole for a bit so he can insert a finger to check if anything suspicious hides inside my ass. What a fuckin nightmare. He then pushed his finger in my asshole, then to the right side, then to the left. Few minutes later told me to take my dick out. He measured it but done by the way it made my nerves jump and the fact that I didn't even want to think how embarrassed made me feel I better shut up. Prison clothing handed out and then taken to a building where I was assigned to a cell. All I wanted is to put my head down on anything and just go to sleep. It was a few hard hours for me that day. Later on after having something to eat, I could hear hundreds prisoners shouting, fighting, all kind of weird stuff, but that was totally normal jail behaviour. That's when it really hit me. The realisation of being in jail. And it was enough to feel the punishment not to return to jail. Then the smell...oh God. A very specific jail smell, something like ammonia or chlorine, seriously ugly smell and that shit smells in the cell too. It's everywhere. Strong and ugly smell. I think I repeated myself at least a hundred times about this jail smell. Experiencing all this crap dally is punishment done well. I made my bed, put my few belongings away, and I start looking out the window to see whatever the fuck was in front of me. The landscape is alright. I get the sea view. Not too bad. Morning came and first night in jail done. Some silence for an hour. Outside still feels like nighttime but is actually more like 5:00 a.m. Then, I hear the guards' clinking of keys getting louder. Finally my door was opened. I stepped out of my cell, trying not to catch everyone's eyes. The first person talked to me was my next cell neighbour. He asked me what am I doing here. I pretended I'm deaf. He kept trying to ask me more questions. Things I don't understand. I think he asked me if I have any sugar and a coil. I ignored him. I was in a crazy people's place so I kept my mouth shut. Now, 85 days in and still don't talk with anyone. Well, I'm confined to this cell and barely I see any humans around. This part of the building is very quiet. I think I'm only myself here, although I sometimes hear some shouting. Don't know from where. Must be some other prisoners. In 15 days it will be all over.

31. 1. 2020: Today it rained the whole afternoon but cleared up just before sunset. Very short day. Daylight shuts down so fast in January. Sea calmer. I can see small fishing boats from my window. I hope they catch something if not God help them with their next catch. Winter fishing in Scotland is quite something especially trout, cold water fish. I have some fantastic memories about winter fishing but not in Scotland, but in jail. Where you can stare at fishing boats from the far end corner of a prison cell. One might interpret this with…"but aren't you in a Scotish jail?" I am indeed.

1. 2. 2020: I caught huge bug under my bed. It was the size of a pack of cigarettes. Black, big eyes, and very hairy. When I tried to catch it, it took off. It start flying all over. Eventually it made its way out the window. Can't believe how huge it was. It must be an alien or

something. Day by day this jail it becomes very strange and I can't wait to get the hell out of it in 14 days. In the evening saw a beautiful winter eagle. All white but with a little yellow patches on his head. He came by my window, and by the way, I'm not sure if this big ass bird was a "he" or a "she" for now I'll just call it "he" or "Mr." there you go, even better, and when he landed it felt more like the moon just landed outside my window, that white he was. I swear on her majesty cedar soap that for a minute the eagle brighten up my cell. As much as I hate colour white never seen in my life such a beauty. I think for a moment I actually enjoyed colour white. Must be an angel sent from God. He then took a good look at me, and he done it from an angle like he was trying to tell me something. In a second it took off like an aircraft. Must be in a hurry. But you not gonna believe what this big ass bird had in his jaw. Huge rat, and it was alive. It was moving. I saw it with my own eyes. He then swallowed the rat in a second and took off. Seriously good meal. Not like me living on tap water and eggs. At least if those eggs were alright. God damn eggs. I hate boiled eggs. I'm so hungry right now that I would eat anything. Even one boiled egg. Dog food...you name. Literally anything. But if they give me dog food I want the one from tails.com, it's my favourite. Comes with 75% great value minced dog food from Hong Kong. It says King Kong on the label. It's my favourite. Jail survival is all about ingenuity. Turning the useless into use. I'll say a few prayers then i can go to sleep.

2. 2. 2020: Hold your breath while i read you today's latest news: I have less than two weeks until I get out of jail and decided I will eat

anything. Bugs. Scorpions. Rats. Even dog food. What's the worse that can happen to me? Nothing worse can happen. I'll just go to heaven. Life is not ended but changed. Problem solved. Going to bed. Actually I changed my mind. I hate that bed. Rusty old iron, bended and full of bed bugs. It's been nearly three months since I last shaved. It will be interesting to see my mug in a mirror after all this time. I'm sure everyone will agree with me I look like a middle age man holding a banana in my left hand. But not because is something wrong to hold a banana but because my banana dried out since I arrived in jail. It's okay, I'm going bananas when I get out. Today i felt something i never felt before. It's about my beard. I have developed a habit to keep scratch it especially around the neck area. I have this constant itchy sensation and it has now become annoying. Sometimes I get under my nails these small insects the size of a needle point. They are so small and jumps out very quickly from one place to another. They look like very tinny bugs and are black. I think are mites because of the way they jump. Very quick motherfuckers. Tried to catch one but it disappeared in nowhere. Usually you get to see mites living on dogs and cats but not on humans. In jail anything is possible. I think it's probably the dog food. Got mites from it. When I get out of jail I will get a full shave and the mites will go out with it. Oh God I'm so hungry I'll eat anything. Hope they bring more dog food. It's high in protein. Speaking about food. You see, one man's faith allows him to eat anything, even dog food, but another man who's faith is weak eats only picky food, low calorie shit, gluten free and salads. Makes you think. Makes you wonder. For this reason I dare you eat anything. Even field mice. Chewed-up paper. Holes in the wall. Jelly bean wires. Mumi's fanny marmalade. Daddy's flower beds. Her majesty cheddar soap. Rabbits at twenty miles per hour. Shredded lupin on brown toast although this is mostly out of stock. 50 Cent gold pennies. One hour microwaved beans. Natural fog. Chilly wind of January. Canned dog food. You see, theres plenty of options. Thank God I like all these. Let me know how you get on. Take two aspirin and tweet me. Going to bed.

3. 2. 2020: Just had the usual soup bowl and things are not so good. Part of my vision is blurry and sometimes I see green. I'm expecting not to die. Terrible weather all day. Some rain. Some snow. Some strong wind. Never seen such strange weather in my jail life. I guess in Scotish jails everything is possible. In the afternoon a strange looking bird came to my window. It almost got inside my celly. I think she wanted to check me out if I'm still alive or not. Who knows maybe this bird was an angel sent from God. Definitely not a devil. She's white. By the way, I'm not sure if this bird was a "she" or a "he" for now and for the readers purpose I will use the pronoun "she" or maybe call this bird "Miss." There you go, even better. Actually, It might be better to say a prayer. "Dear God & Father of all heavens, can you send me a bird trap so I can catch this big ass bird and eat it alive? Because I'm so hungry and my faith is not so good these days. Thanks a lot. Saint Isaac from cell number 13." I was staying in bed waiting for my wish from God but in the same time watching this big ass bird how she's staring at me and it almost hypnotised me. You know something? Sometimes in life there are moments when life itself imitates art. Right now I feel like I'm into one

of those moments. Inevitably we will all somehow face it and it will come like a thoroughly unpleasant opportunity to take part of it. I mean c'mon...look what is happening to me. I'm living my worst part of literature and there's also this big ass bird staring at me. It kinda intimidates me. Maybe I shod search for answers into one of those self-help books, it will probably help me...actually I think self-help books are the biggest disease right now, it reminds you so fuckin often how difficult everything is. Makes you so fuckin low. And if you are one of those self-help authors don't ask me to take my words back, retract a statement I previously made or such thing. I'm in jail. I must bitch about something otherwise is no normal day for me. Holly crap, my jail food just arrived. Pack of biscuits and half mouldy bread. One million tweets please.

4. 2. 2020: Some good news today. I received official jail correspondence and it is signed and dated by the governor. The paper says I will definitely be released on the 15th of this month. That will be in eleven days from today. Let's make it ten from tomorrow because today is almost midday. I will have my jail food and go straight for bed to make things go faster. Imagine doing this from the first day I arrived in these premises, jail time would go so much faster. Instead, I complained every day until it made my world a constant depression. I nearly forgot how is to be happy. Just want to sit quiet on a bench, somewhere in a park, facing a nice lake, perhaps seeing a few ducks playing. Feed the pigeons. I want a nice blow of sun on my skin and I want to be free to do whatever I want. This jail experience has been too much for me. Way too much. It

nearly killed my mental health. Sometimes I feel like I live into a constant scandal with my thoughts. Just terrifying. Might have to sign up with one of those mindfulness apps to calm down my brain. I shall see when I get out. It will be alright. Ten more days and I'm out. Beautiful afternoon today. Sunny & clean, almost no win. It feels like spring outside. Going to bed in the middle of the day it's so annoying when I know there's so much to be enjoyed out there...yeah right... here I am, locked in here. I swear to God when I get out of jail I ain't sleep a day until I die. So much to catch up. Just so much.

5. 2. 2020: Woke up in a freezing cold bed. I really don't get it, yesterday was alright, I almost thought spring came, today definitely winter. Bipolar looking weather. Another example why It's not wrong to say the weather is bipolar. And for someone who has no clue what the word bipolar means, it's perfectly normal. I'm sure there will be people who read this and think "...but aren't you bipolar?" In a nutshell I have poor Wi-Fi connection to research my diagnosis so I will just stick with the weather. Another strange bird keeps coming back at my window. This one it's the size of a pigeon. All white. Has large wings, long legs, a very long bony mouth. Seems to be one of those angel birds from the bible. "Lord, is it you? Did you came to bring me communion?" I asked nicely but didn't answered. Must be deaf or something. By the way, last night I had a dream...rather strange looking dream. I was part of a Big Brother Tv show and was given a tour of the Big Brother house and in the middle of the house there was a little garden. Nice flowers, bees flying around, yes, you heard that, bees, and these were green bees the size of a coin, more

like alien style bees, so there I was stuck in the middle of the garden then suddenly from nowhere the garden transformed itself into a shower. I was under the shower with three naked women and whats even more strange was the water that came from the shower. Well, it was not actual water, it was milk but the milk it didn't came from the shower. The milk came from these women's breasts, each one pumping out their breast milk on each other. They've been having a lot of fun, myself had to do the cleaning after them otherwise they would expel me from Big Brother. I'm telling you, I had some very strange dreams in this jail. I could probably write "Blood And Guts In Jail V2.0" only with ideas from dreams. I already done a few short stories based on dreams I've had in this jail, but the biggest thing I've found is that things that seem to make sense in dreams don't really work so much when you wake up. As such, the dreams usually end up being a seed idea and not a literal step-by-step story. When I was at the jail hospital I wrote away from the dream, but still, it was the seed that started it, so it served its purpose, which was getting me to write again all kind of Imaginary stories, some from dreams and some from jail. I'm going back to sleep to look for more imaginary things and hopefully a new story will come out tomorrow, otherwise, if I stay awake I will virtually bitch anything I see in front of me. I'm in jail. I must bitch about something otherwise is no normal day for me.

6. 2. 2020: Today constantly thinking I have nine days to go until I get out of jail. Is it a real thing? Well, it says on the calendar that 15 of February 2020 is in nine days so it must be real to me and fictional to the author. Now here's the funny part and this is not

fictional at all. This is real life happening in nine days from now. I get out of jail and have nowhere to go. My situation is pretty much straight forward...I'm 30 years old, I haven't got a pot to piss in, I'm broke, I have no family, no friends, definitely no one to ask for help when I get out, but I have a couple of bitcoin in my saving account... and that shod get me closer to one hundred grand. So...is not too bad. That should suffice for now. One thing that really annoys me is living with a criminal record for writing a book behind bars. That's like a permanent tattoo on my forehead. But there is hope. My passion for writing and mixing records it will prove an instant hit. Only minds who reinvent themselves succeed. I believe there is a way to follow my dreams. I keep dreaming.

7.2.2020: I really don't know what else to write but I know I have eight more days until I get out. I could probably write about the stuff I want to do on the outside. Already made myself a list of what I will order for my first lunch when I'm out. That will be a good start. I shall have the cottage pie please, and I know I sound like I already order, but give me some time to think, and I'm also gonna have huge jar of gravy and I'll drink that shit like a slug to remind me how good life is. Actually, what constitute a good life? A good life can be described as a life that is self-satisfying and self-fulfilling. So I shall self-fulfill myself by adding more to my order. Home made chips please, the chunky ones, and I want them on a wooden board to remind me of my chef days...Yes people, I use to scrap pots for minimum wage, but it was chips that got me thru those sixteen hours long shifts. I use to pick them up from wooden boards. You know, leftovers. And I also want to burn 800 calories but not on a treadmill, but by licking an ice cream. You will be silly not to know what I mean. You know what I mean. Yes you know what I mean. Yes, it's a been a while. Ice cream please. Today's whether it's not too bad. Looking really good. Nice blow of sun all over my arm and it feels so good. Love the feeling. On a good day when the sky is clean from clouds I get a good chunk of sun into my cell. And when that happens I close my eyes and lift up my arms to get the blow. It kinda lifts up my spirits. This pinch of happiness it really hits my weakest spot. I'm now emotional. Hopefully one day I will be able to make a great return. Eight more days to go and I'm out. Night...night.

8. 2. 2020: What is going on here? Yesterday it felt like spring came into my cell. Today it feels like I'm living in hell. The most far hell you could imagine, one of those upper hells at the top of the globe. Like the one from the north pole. If there would be such a thing. Very cold today. Polar style wind and it bites like rats. And rats always like to bite by the face. This cold wind stings. I ain't sign up for this shit. I gave this wind a nickname, "kissing wind" and I name it this way for a rather unpleasant reason...it stresses the shit out of my last days in jail. I swear to God on my liberation day I will piss all over the place and I will start with the bed. At least it will kill the bed bugs. That much I hate this jail. Need to calm down. One more week and I'm out.

9. 2. 2020: I haven't got out of bed just yet. Theres strange weather happening outside. Blows of wind, some snow, plenty of rain, quite a bit of ice and it comes in tiny pieces, very sharp ones. Never seen this type of weather. Some of that is coming thru a shitty hole in the wall. It supposed to be my window. I removed it the other day so I can get more air. Sometimes the jail smell it breaks me down to pieces but it won't kill me, I will survive this hell. Plus, hell is for heroes. It's interesting how the weather it changes so fast. Only two days ago I was enjoying a blow of sun on my arms. Not anymore. The jail roof is doing strange noises. I've been hearing the damn thing all night long. I think is from the wind. Definitely from the wind. In the beginning I thought are ghosts, far from the sea. Then I thought are mermaids trying to have a conversation with me. But I also thought It's someone beating a goat and a donkey in the same

time. I actually love donkeys, I use to ride one in my childhood. Hopefully the wind will blow the shit out of it. The jail roof not the donkey. My food just arrived. The usual tray with the usual boring stuff. But I need to eat something to stay strong and get out alive. Jail days in the winter time are no joke. Time for a shit meal.

10. 2. 2020: Even more bad weather and today is no joke. Plenty of rain, snow, and very strong wind. Never seen such strange weather. The sea looks angry with plenty of breakers. I really don't get it, three days ago it was like spring came into my cell. Now, five more days to go until I get out and I'm living my worst time in jail. Gosh I'm tired of keep complaining about all kind of shit. I really want to think of something positive, some beautiful thoughts. Anything really. Woke up with terrible pain on my back. The bed frame is bent and it affects my back. It's an old structube bed frame that keeps bending in the middle of the night. When I try to get a good night sleep this motherfucker ruins my sleep. It's either the bed or the bed bugs or sometimes both. Theres a can of chicken noodle soup standing on the table. I hope is real. It was just there when I woke up. I think one of the prison guards put it while I was sleeping because I don't remember having a can of chicken noodle in my cell. At least for the past 95 days. It looks like a good meal. I ate it in five seconds and it was so good. This might be my liberation day prize. Wait! You wanna hear something fucked-up? Five minutes later I fished the thing out of the bin and realised it was not a can of chicken noodle soup but an empty roll of toilet paper. I must be going insane. I now know I start seeing things that are not real. I don't think even this

book is real. Don't you think? If you think is real then take two
aspirin and tweet me. Tell me what you think because right now I
have a hard time to think about anything. Oh man...I barely walk. My
bones hurts so bad. I'm nearly 100 days in jail and i already feel 10
more years older. At least if not more. I really feel old. Tired at all
times. Dirty. Smelly. Ugly. All three at once. It's an awful feeling to
live with for 100 days. Today I noticed something out of the corner
of my eye. It hurts when I touch it. Probably a bunch of insects bitten
me in my sleep. It's no surprise these creature are bed bugs.
Definitely bed bugs. I'm hoping I will not get an eye infection. It's the
last thing I need on my liberation day. Getting out blind. I ain't sign up
for this shit anyway. Outside still the same weather. Nothing
changed but just the wind direction. Wish I could have heat on
constantly. Actually, I wish I can forget all my troubles under a
bucket of hot water. I really do need one. It will heal my body. I start
to have these uncontrolled tremors all over my body and it's not
stoping. Can't keep it under control unless I fall asleep. And I can
barely sleep because of the cold. For the past few days I've been up
all night, only a little sleep during the day. I don't like that. I'm a light
sleeper. Almost anything wakes me up. And I have difficulty sleeping
through noise. But if I get tired enough, my body will command that I
sleep in conditions I wouldn't normally be able to sleep through and
eventually I will fall asleep. I wish I could have slept through my entire
fuckin sentence and don't even think I'm in jail. At least I got my
zzzz's in for life. So the answer is no, I did not had a good sleep in
jail. Most of the time is loud, scary noises coming from all over the
place, cold, ugly, miserable fuckin jail. But I'm in jail anyway so I
better get used to it at least for the next five more days. They don't

even open the door anymore, instead, someone pushes my food tray thru food-flap. The food passes through and thats it, is left there on the floor. This usually happens when I'm asleep. By the time I wake up to eat it it's freezing cold, but I don't care anyway because it tastes like shit. Five more days and I'm out.

11. 2. 2020: My last days in jail are like years of sweat on my forehead. I don't even have enough tissues how much sweat I carry with me. It's like carrying the sun in a golden cup. Damn weather. It messes with my head. In less than a week this whole movie comes to an end but if my readers are begging for more it's all good, they can catch me in my next episode..."Blood And Guts Before I Die." Don't worry I won't die, instead, I will be making a great comeback and my future will be bright. I swear I won't return to jail even if will be less of me. When I'm out I will just take the first left until I hit dead end and will do it with a backpack. Prison is like an amputation. You die. You live again. No one recognises your struggles. The day begins to raise and I have that smartness in my eyes that comes from being up all night. I'm five days in until the final. Barely I think of any sleep. Looking out the window, mainland almost invisible because of so much snow. Strange weather keeps going. Last night I've been thinking all night long what shod I do when I get out. Here's four things that came to my mind. First thing to do is erase my heroine. I don't plan to take her with me in my next book. I don't like her attitude. She's a first class tough cookie. Strong enough to piss me off. My next book is all about me and my journey to somewhere. Don't know yet where. Second, whatever is on the menu at the pub

around the corner I will take it. I'm hungry for some good food. Third, whatever brings tomorrow I will write about it. Fourth, become an interesting person. I've always been told by so many people that I'm some kind of interesting person. So maybe I shod think about that and become windswept & interesting. But become a bit more. I always knew I'm an interesting person until I got the jail. Look! I wrote a book. Interesting isn't it? I hope you like it. It's not really difficult to become an interesting person. You just have to be it. Then people will kinda notice that you are. Interesting people recognise each other. It's not really about what you wear or how much money you have, it's more of a behaviour thing. Some kind of attitude of the mind. Also the environment the interesting person lives. For example, before getting the jail I had this small apartment, and by the way, it pisses me off just to think I lost everything...my recording studio, yes, I had an amazing recording studio. And my vinyl record collection, hundreds of books....oh man, it hurts when I think I get out of jail and none of that I will see it again. The fuckin landlord wrote me a letter the other day saying he binned all my stuff. Motherfucker. I hope he farts spaghetti Bolognese. I better don't think about this right now otherwise I may suffer an existential crisis with my life. Yes, I was talking about this windswept & interesting thing. Interesting people are surrounded by things they like, musical instruments, record collections, lots of books, sketchbooks, drawings, paintings, hats, shirts decorated with flowers, assorted scarves, a nice handbag, a fancy perfume or perhaps a few perfumes, a stylish mix of objects. That's just how interesting people live. All my life I've been living that way, surrounded by a few of these interesting things. Until I got the jail. Fuck the past. I will try to feel brilliant from my first freedom day and behave accordingly...like a windswept & interesting person. Damn it, it's so cold in my cell. Polar style weather and has no plans to stop. Today I imagined myself like in one of those soviet style jails from the first world war. It was quite dark and I was sitting alone on this ugly chair. Looking at nothing but thinking at something. And there was this blue light reflecting on the walls and it was coming from the evening glaze. I'm not making this up. This was quite an interesting moment. Then a small cloud of fog came over me. But it was my own air from my lungs. The air in my lungs is warm and moist, but the air outside is very cold. I think it's called condensation and is responsible for the formation of clouds. I then start exhaling fog all over the place and my cell turned into a stage before filming a horror movie. You get the background. More jail memories tomorrow. It's time for me to say good night.

12. 2. 2020: Good morning ya all & howareyoudoing today? I'm fine, thanks for asking. I have excellent news. I just received a soap. Around midday, a jail guard opened the cell and told me it's time to get the wash. "Sure, why not" I said. I got the wash today. It was really good to hold a soap in my hand. A miracle. And it looked really nice. I'm sure it's made from dead animal grease, kidneys and loins of cattle, sheep, and horses but I got the wash and I still stink. It's probably from dead animal grease but I trust the process. On the pack it says it adds a protective layer on your skin. I'm very grateful. Round two to follow in late afternoon and this is called "kit change." I've been told they let me shave. The sad truth is when I see my mug

in a mirror for the first time in 100 days it will turn my stomach upside down. I rarely seen good looking Saint Isaac in jail.

13. 2. 2020: A much better day today. Not because I'm out in two days but because the sky is perfectly clear. Nice blue sky and a touch of sun happens right now. No more ugly weather. It's like God wants to show me the way. Hopefully the way out. Enjoying this blow of sun on my arms. It feels really good although still cold. Gosh I would love an espresso. "One espresso for here please." Don't worry, I'm just talking with myself. And I want it warm, not too hot, and I also want to sip some sparkling water. Finally, I want to sip and enjoy. Now I know how to drink espresso. Don't worry, I'm just imagining. Washing myself in the sink was a fuckin nightmare. I remember quite clearly only the cold. Oh dear, I shaken for the rest of the day. I actually regret getting the wash. It felt more like an attempted suicide rather than an actual wash. Never in my life I felt that cold. It was about mid-day when I got the wash, and it was with cold water. The coldest water you'll ever get. For the rest of the day and the full night I literally shaken. It's been a few hours since I start calming down a little. I think the feeling of getting out of jail is what keeps me alive. To be honest the only reason I didn't bother to get a wash for so long it's because of the cold. Instead I preferred to wear the same ugly jail clothes for almost 100 days. Some days it kept me warm. Some not. Just had my bowl of soup. It's crap food but it's fine. Evening seems finer but cold. Sea not so rough. More like just after the storm. It just settles down. Damn it, can't believe I'm out in a couple of days. It kinda puts me back on the mood. A cheerful

mood. For the past few days I become a melancholic fool. I miss my life so much. Back home I have a room dedicated only for my record library. Nice looking shelfs filled with hundreds of vinyl records and I miss the vintage smell of my vinyls. They tend to have a very characteristic smell. Odd in the beginning but pleasant the more you smell it. Maybe is because most of them are decades old. I miss my small kitchen and the smell of toast at exactly 5:00 a.m. Got this habit to always wake up early to get stuff done. Doing some writing, some reading, quite a bit of planing, sometimes producing a piece of music in the early morning. I was getting so much done because of this habit to wake up early. By 11:00 a.m all jobs were done. Well, I don't want to call them jobs. It was something I love doing. Theres an old saying that If you do what you love, you'll never work a day in your life. Something like that. And by 11:30 a.m I was out and about, free to do whatever I want. I also miss my awesome clothing. I tend to have the habit of placing each garment in a specific place, in a specific style, ironed, cleaned, so they can always look fresh. As you can see I used to have quite a few interesting things around my home but not any more. Thanks to my landlord it's now all gone. Motherfucker, he binned all my stuff to vacate the flat. I will try to move on and never think about it. The last thing I want is to get into an existential crisis with my life. With pennies in the pocket I will build everything back and this time I will do it right. Gotta keep an open mind. Cheers to chips and gravy. A strange and characteristically gothic moon is happening right now on the big sky. So red. So boldly. I'm sure the moon's reflection on the ocean's surface is even visible from the international space station. I know this may sound strange but on a good night it's actually a romantic view from my window. I get a full view of the sea. Sometimes it looks like a postcard. If the northern lights kicks in then it's definitely a postcard. Getting tired and bored. Nothing else to do but just force myself to sleep.

14. 2. 2020: Diaries are books too. Originally this book was a diary with the intention to record everything from how much water I drink to the food I ate and everything else in between life in jail. But when jail life kicked in, this diary became something else, something more personal. It become my best friend for 100 days and it also made me strong enough to realise things around my cell and face them. Things like loneliness and depression and sometimes bed bugs. I had to face my demons. You have no idea what is going on behind the scenes of this jail. Well, I didn't cry after all cause I am raw and naked soul and I want to stay real for all of you, with my weakness and power. And when it hurts - it hurts. I put it down on words. I am not complaining, just reporting on my current state of mind. I am in jail today but not anymore tomorrow. Wish you a great day guys. I'm on my way to tomorrow. And please think of this book as "The Diary of Saint Isaac." The convict not the missionary.

15. 2. 2020: I'm out. See you in my next book and I'll tell you more about.

Not...THE END

Postscript

Blood And Gus In Jail is an amazing story. It is a truly great memoir. But it can also sounds very personal. More like a real story and the more you read the more you think like..."What in the hell is going on here. Is it the Writer who experienced all this?" Indeed it feels very real everything you read in this book. I truly wanted to write something that people will want to read, and the only way to make it happen was to act like actually happened. To act like everything was real. For that I become an actor myself, Isaac Bjorn the author of the book. I never seen myself an actor, yet I had to put myself in the shoes of the character and become him — "Saint Isaac." I had to take a few hours of acting classes, learn the basics of script writing, learn how to create compelling plots, strong hooks, learn how to build an argument for the existence of fictional characters, and I even had to read books on Behavioural Psychology. I also had to learn about jail life in generally, and to do that I had to interview a few former prisoners. It help me understand jail life a little better. From there it was the product of my imagination. I had to learn the ins & outs about all these so I can build very strong hooks in the book, and make it sound very real even if everything is purely fictional. As you probably seen in the book, the character, adventure himself every day profoundly different. In an imaginary world of his own he start documenting his thoughts on paper. He calls it "his diary." He truly wants to becomes a writer in his cell, daily hustling using nothing but just pen and paper and the product of his imagination. He also has a goal, wants to finish his book by the time his sentence is finished. He has no idea what to write about, but soon he began to write about his complex issues and jail life was his drive. He start arguing with imaginary characters, sometimes building relationships with them and sometimes entering in conflicts with them. He also creates a heroine. The love of his life, but she never existed, only being the product of his imagination. It was a very difficult book to write. It took me exactly two months plus an additional two on editing the whole manuscript. Produced during the end of UK lockdown pandemic. Thank you for reading my book. I do hope I did not offended anyone. The story is purely fiction. This has been Isaac Bjorn. The Author of Blood And Guts In Jail.

ABOUT THE AUTHOR

Isaac Bjorn is the author of "Blood And Guts In Jail" & "Blood And Guts Before I Die." Host of "Isaac Bjorn Talk Show" on Spotify & Apple Podcasts, also Record Producer & DJ under the alias PLANETBJORN. These days Isaac works as Personal Development Consultant at isaacbjorn.com, helping people unlock their creative life potential on a self help basis. He provides a plan, idea, advice. He lives in Glasgow, Great Britain.

🐦 Isaac_Bjorn

📷 isaacbjorn

f IsaacBjornOfficial

🌐 www.isaacbjorn.com

Printed in Great Britain
by Amazon